Apple Island

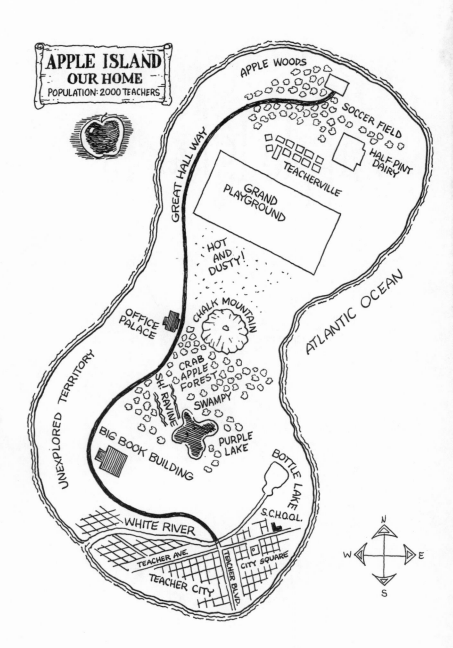

Apple Island
or The Truth About Teachers

Douglas Evans

pictures by
Larry Di Fiori

Front street
Asheville, North Carolina
1998

for Brian Evans

Library of Congress Cataloging-in-Publication Data
Evans, Douglas, 1953—
Apple Island, or, the truth about teachers
Douglas Evans; illustrated by Larry Di Fiori. — 1st ed.
p.   cm.
Summary: When Bradley and his class are taken on an unexpected field trip
to Apple Island, he discovers a group of evil teachers plotting to take over
the schools of America and "misteach" all the children.
ISBN 1-886910-25-1 (alk. paper)
[1. Teachers—Fiction. 2. Humorous Stories.]
I. Di Fiori, Lawrence, ill. II. Title
PZ7.E8775Ap   1997
[Fic]—dc21   97-9373

Contents

The School Day Begins

"She's a crabby old fat lady who hasn't taught us a thing! I hate teachers! I hate school!" Bradley announced as he trudged toward that very place one October morning.

The sun was up, but not far enough up to warm the chilly air. Puffs of steam shot from Bradley's mouth as he spoke.

"Boring, boring, boring! That's what school is. I wish all teachers and schools would disappear forever!"

Duncan, Bradley's friend and classmate, strutted two steps ahead, trying to pick up the pace. "School is school

and teachers are teachers," he said. "And since we have to go to school we'd better hurry or we'll be late. Nothing makes the teacher crabbier than when kids are tardy."

Bradley stomped on a pill bug that had the misfortune of crossing his path. "But Mrs. Gross is crabby all the time," he said. "The only time you see her smile is when she's dishing out punishments. You do one little thing wrong, like forget your homework, and she screams her head off."

"Mrs. Gross is new at our school," said Duncan. "Maybe she'll get better. Who knows?"

Bradley reached around and slapped his backpack. "And think what books she makes us read. Boring! And the math sheets she makes us do. Just problem after problem of the same boring stuff."

"What about story writing?" asked Duncan. "Mrs. Gross puts a gold star on all my papers."

"She flunks everything I write," Bradley said. "She says I'll never be a good writer since my handwriting and spelling are so bad. I don't think she even reads my stories."

The boys stopped at a street corner. A woman wearing an orange vest marched out to the middle of the street. She held up a stop sign on a stick, and a yellow school bus squealed to a halt. Bradley and Duncan strode by the woman, forgetting to stay within the crosswalk.

"I wonder where Mrs. Gross lives," Bradley mused. "Where does any teacher live? Do they cook and do housecleaning? I can't imagine teachers doing anything normal."

"Teachers are teachers," Duncan repeated.

The pair walked through a gate in the chain-link fence that surrounded the school grounds.

BRRRIIIIIIIIIIIIIIIIIIIING!

The morning bell sounded across the playground. From all directions students streamed toward the beige, L-shaped school building. The American flag flying from the flagpole waved good morning to them.

As Duncan ran ahead, Bradley stopped to slug a tetherball and watch it twirl around the pole.

"It's Monday," he said. "Eight hours until the day's over. Five days until the week is through. Twenty-seven weeks until the year's over, and eight years until I graduate. School! Who invented it? Why is it here? I hate teachers! I hate everything about school!"

In class

Bradley shuffled into the classroom. After dumping his jacket on the floor of the coat closet, he slunk into his seat in the third row. He frowned at the WELCOME BACK TO SCHOOL sign still on the bulletin board. He scowled at the empty aquarium on the counter. He glowered at the blank walls and bare bookshelf. He shook his head at the blackboard filled with long, tedious sentences to copy, and then he checked the clock above it.

Turning, he said to Duncan behind him, "One hour and forty-eight minutes until recess."

In front of the blackboard, behind a large metal desk, sat the teacher, Mrs. Gross, in a large swivel chair. Even though the desk hid most of the teacher's tremendous bulk, Bradley could see the width of her shoulders, the thickness of her neck, and the flabbiness of her cheeks.

The chinless face, the squinty eyes, and a thick lower lip pushed out in a permanent scowl reminded him of an overripe apple.

The teacher coughed into her fist, smudging her red lipstick. She lifted a coffee mug off her desk and took a long slug. After patting her puffy brown hairdo, she picked up the attendance book.

"Morning, stooodents," she said in a raspy voice that caught everyone's attention immediately. "Say 'Here' when I call your name. Not 'Present.' Not 'Yes.' Only 'Here.' Understand? Good. Now we begin . . . Celeste-Marie Aardvark!"

"Here," peeped a small girl in the back row.

Bradley slumped in his chair as far as he could without slipping off. One quick look around the classroom told him that the entire class was present, but he didn't mind this daily chance to daydream before schoolwork began.

"Why did Mrs. Gross ever become a teacher?" he asked himself. "She seems to hate kids. She seems to hate being at this school. I wonder how she became a teacher. Teachers! I'll never figure them out."

"Bradley Zimmerman!" Mrs. Gross's voice thundered.

Bradley jerked straight up in his seat. "Present," he piped out.

The teacher gave him a frightening scowl before dashing off a final check in her attendance book. She took another long gulp of coffee and wiped her lips with the back of her hand.

"Good, stooodents," she said. "Everyone is here today." Pushing her knuckles onto the desktop, she slowly stood. "Time for mathematics!"

The classroom filled with the usual groans and gripes following this announcement. Yet before anyone took out a math book, Mrs. Gross said something extraordinary. "No need for books today, stooodents. No need for pencils and paper. Today we are going to learn a new type of math. And since the math we have been learning was a new form of the new math, we shall call this math the New New New Math."

The students stared at her in stunned silence. Not only had Mrs. Gross's announcement been a shock, but now a rare smile spread across her face.

The teacher straightened her dress over her chubby legs and stepped in front of the desk. She picked a large card off her desktop and held it up for all to see:

$$6 \times 9$$

"Looky here, stooodents," she said, continuing to grin. "See what I have. A big flashcard. And see what the flash-

card says, six times nine. Now can anybody tell me, what does six times nine equal?"

A hand shot up in the front row and waved frantically back and forth like a windshield wiper set on double speed.

Mrs. Gross pointed a sausage finger at a boy with a face full of freckles and shiny braces. "Yeeeees, Errol," she called.

"Six times nine equals fifty-four," the boy spouted out.

"Yeeeees, Errol," said Mrs. Gross. "That is absolutely correct. Did everyone hear Errol? Did everyone notice how Errol is paying attention and raised his hand before answering? Good boy, Errol."

Errol turned in his seat and flashed a silvery grin toward his classmates.

Bradley squinted at the boy. "Teacher's pet," he muttered. Errol was a show-off. Errol was a tattletale. Errol had gotten Bradley in trouble many times. Bradley despised him.

"Now, stooodents," said Mrs. Gross. "Pay close attention. Watch what I do."

With a great deal of ceremony she turned the flashcard upside down. It still read:

$$6 \times 9$$

"Now, stooodents, tell me the answer."

Several voices repeated, "Fifty-four!"

Mrs. Gross's thick lips spread wider. "Remember, stooodents, this is the New New New Math," she said. "Six times nine right side up equals fifty-four. Upside down, it equals forty-five."

In the third row, Bradley, who had been daydreaming, sat bolt upright at his desk. What? What did the teacher say?

Mrs. Gross held up a second flashcard:

$$1 \times 1$$

"What is the answer, stooodents?" she asked.

"One!" the class chorused.

"But . . . ," said Mrs. Gross. Again she turned the card upside down. "Now it equals eleven! So you see, stooodents, in the New New New Math any problem that looks the same right side up as upside down has two answers. This is true with eleven times eleven, sixteen times ninety-one, and so forth. Any questions? Good. That is all the mathematics for today."

Bradley sat in his seat without moving. What was going

on? Everything the teacher just said was wrong. The New New New Math made no sense at all. He waited for a classmate to say something, but no one did. Bradley couldn't help himself. Something deep inside him demanded that he speak up. "But . . . but . . . that's ridiculous!" he blurted out.

A hush fell over the classroom. Everyone stared at Mrs. Gross. Her smile collapsed. She clasped her hands behind her grand behind and rocked back on her heels. One thick eyebrow crept up her forehead as she glared at Bradley in the third row.

"Well, Mr. Zimmerman," she said. "Well, well, well, well, well. So you think mathematics is ridiculous, eh?"

Bradley's armpits grew hot. "No," he said. "It's just hard to believe that the answer changes just because you turned the flashcard upside down."

Mrs. Gross smiled around the room. "Well, well, well. Just listen to Bradley, stooodents," she said. "He thinks he knows more about math than the teacher does. He thinks he is a math wizard or something."

Snickers surrounded Bradley.

He felt a tap on his shoulder. "Come off it, Bradley," Duncan whispered. "The teacher said math was over, so it's over."

Before Bradley could say another word, Mrs. Gross had turned toward the blackboard and grabbed a piece of chalk. "Time for spelling, stooodents," she announced. "And guess what? Spelling has also changed."

Her chalk squeaked against the board as she wrote a list of words:

com
giv
hav
frend
ci

"You see, stooodents, teachers have made spelling easier for you. Dictionaries are incorrect. All those nasty silent letters in words are preposterous! From now on you can leave off the silly *e* at the end of *come*, *give*, and *have*. Forget that idiotic *i* in the middle of *friend*. Why bother putting the dumb *b* at the end of *climb*? And never write *phone* with a *ph* or *laugh* with a *gh* again. Enough already! If you hear an *f*, just put an *f*!"

Again Bradley spoke before he could stop himself. "But you can't change spelling like that! No one would understand what you were writing."

Groans filled the air. Duncan let out a long sigh.

Mrs. Gross spun around and pointed her chalk at Bradley. "Doubting the teacher again, eh, Mr. Zimmerman? And since when are you such a fine speller? Eh? I do believe you fail every spelling test I give. In fact, Mr. Zimmerman, you flunk most things in this class. I've rarely seen such little ability in any stooodent. And, dear boy, report cards are coming out next week. Not a good time to question the teacher. Eh? No, no, not a good time. I'll have to make a note of this."

By this time sweat was dripping down Bradley's forehead. He wanted to speak out again, but the teacher's frightening glare kept him silent.

Next Mrs. Gross pulled down the map above the blackboard. At once Bradley saw that this map was different. It showed the normal outlines of the United States, but within the borders more black lines had been added.

"Now, stooodents," said the teacher. "If there are no more interruptions, I will teach you about the seventy states in the United States of America."

At that moment the recess bell rang. The teacher turned and said, "You have done an excellent job this morning, stooodents. Now please remember, the things I taught you this morning are very new. Your parents won't understand them. Perhaps it is best not to talk about anything you learn in school from now on. Understand? Good. Class dismissed."

The Teachers' Lounge

The students filed down the hall toward the playground door. Bradley walked with his hands in his jacket pockets, eyes on Duncan's head in front of him. "Did you hear what the teacher was trying to feed us, Dunc?" he said. "That New New New Math made no sense at all."

"Math never makes sense to me," Duncan replied.

"But I'm telling you, something strange is going on. The teacher is teaching us wrong things. I don't mean like in the old days, when teachers taught that the earth was flat or that the sun traveled around the earth. Back then they didn't know any better. No, Mrs. Gross is teaching us wrong stuff, and she's doing it on purpose."

"Come off it, Bradley," said Duncan. "It's recess time. You're supposed to forget about learning and teachers for ten minutes."

Bradley, however, was in no mood for playground games. He slowed his pace to let the rest of the class go on without him. As he passed his last-year's classroom, he looked in longingly at Miss Purdy, the greatest teacher in the world. Why couldn't all teachers be caring, smart, and funny like Miss Purdy? His former teacher must have just told one of her great jokes, because a blast of laughter came out of the room as Bradley moved down the hall.

"How can some teachers be so kind and others so crabby?" he asked himself. "Something strange is going on with my teacher, and I'm going to find out what it is."

At the drinking fountain he took three slurps of water. He nodded to the janitor, who was washing sponges in his small room that smelled of ammonia. Farther down the hall he stepped into the library to say hello to the librarian in his soft library voice, then waved to the school secretary through the office window.

He stopped before the next door. The black words stenciled on it read:

"I've passed this room hundreds of times since kindergarten, but I've never been inside," Bradley said to himself. "In fact, I've never seen any kid go in there."

He put his ear to the door. Hearing nothing, he leaned forward and the door opened a crack. He checked up and down the hallway, then slipped into the room.

What struck Bradley first about the Teachers' Lounge was the mess. He made a face at the counters cluttered with wads of paper towels, Styrofoam cups, thumbtacks, half-eaten bagels, newspapers, coffee grounds, eraser crumbs, broken crayons, felt markers, pencil shavings, cupcake wrappers, gold glitter, and reams of paper.

"Look at this dump," he said. "And teachers tell us to keep our rooms clean!"

The room smelled of coffee and Magic Marker. A five-gallon coffeemaker hissed on a table. Announcements about substitutes, assemblies, parties, and special meetings were scribbled on a large white board.

In one corner stood an impressive-looking Xerox machine. Bradley lowered his face onto the glass top and pressed the COPY button. Out came a picture of his squishy nose and cheeks.

"I've always wanted to do that," he said. With a blue felt marker he wrote I WAS HERE on the paper and left it on the counter, certain that no teacher could recognize his mashed face.

On the back wall of the room hung a map. It showed a peanut-shaped island, and the extraordinary words printed along one side caught Bradley's immediate attention:

"Apple Island?" he said aloud. "Is that map for real? How could there be an island inhabited only by teachers?"

Suddenly he heard voices in the hall and the door began to swing open. With the lightning reflexes that had won him many games of four-square on the playground, he dove under a counter. He curled up by a stack of old textbooks just as two pairs of legs stopped inches from his face.

One pair of legs, thick, with black knee socks, Bradley recognized at once. He mouthed the words "Mrs. Gross."

The second pair was a mystery. Through her thick nylon stockings, he could see that this woman's ankles were stained purple.

The woman with purple ankles spoke first. "So! This is it, Miss Eraser, typical school, on a typical school day, in a typical American city."

Coffee splattered on the tile floor by Bradley's nose.

"It's been a great honor to have such a distinguished visitor in our schooool today, Head Teacher," came his teacher's voice. "But, please, in this building call me Mrs. Gross. That's what the stooodents call me. Hee hee! Mrs. Gross."

"Indeed, Mrs. Gross," said the first woman. "And today it was super to see typical schoolwork being done by typical small creatures. So! What did you call them again?"

"Children, kids, youngsters, or juveniles. Some are called boys, some girls. At school you call them pupils or stooodents. Collectively they are called a class."

"Whatever they are called, they are messy, giggly things,"

said the lady with purple ankles. "They know so little. Their heads are filled with nonsense. They constantly ask why, why, why and they never stop fidgeting. Some squirm in their chairs even when the teacher is giving a beautiful long lecture. And these juveniles get excited at the silliest things. I observed one boy on your typical playground chase a butterfly and one girl squeal with delight when she caught a lizard. Ridiculous."

"But that's the beauty of Operation Misteach, Head Teacher," said Mrs. Gross. "Children will believe anything teachers tell them. We can mold them like clay in our hands."

"So! How did your class react to Operation Misteach on the first day?"

"Beoootifully, Head Teacher," Mrs. Gross answered.

"Any troublemakers?"

"Only one, Head Teacher. A whining, sniveling boy named Bradley Zimmerman. He asked many questions. He questioned my answers. Luckily none of the other stooodents listen to him. They snicker at him. Hee hee! I gave him the old report-card threat, and that I believe will keep his trap shut. We will have no more trouble from Mr. Zimmerman."

"So! You've done well, Miss Eras—Mrs. Gross," said the woman with purple ankles. "I'm looking forward to this afternoon. Shhh! Here come the other teachers."

The Teachers' Lounge door swung open. Soon Bradley was peering through a forest of teachers' legs.

"What was that conversation all about?" he asked himself. "Who's that Head Teacher? What's Operation Misteach? What's going to happen this afternoon?"

With a dozen chatting, coffee-swigging teachers surrounding him, he rested his head on a book and waited for the end-of-recess bell to ring.

The Field Trip

Back in the classroom, Bradley slipped into his seat. He turned and whispered to Duncan, "Something really weird is going on in this school."

Duncan shrugged. "So what's new?" he said. "You've been saying that all year."

Mrs. Gross or Miss Eraser or whatever her name was stood before the blackboard with her hefty arms folded across her large bosom. Still wearing the unfamiliar grin, she said, "Guess what, stooodents? No more schoolwork today. You are in for a big surprise. We are going on a field trip. That's right, our first field trip of the year. A bus is waiting out front for us right now. Don't ask where we are going. It's a surprise. Any questions? Good. Now get your wraps and line up at the door."

Any other day Bradley would have been ecstatic about going on a field trip. Yet after what he had overheard in the Teachers' Lounge, he slunk to the coat closet shaking his head, full of doubts.

Mrs. Gross led her class down the hall with a surprising amount of bounce in her step. "Come along, come along, stooodents," she sang out. "Oh, you'll find this field trip most amuuuuusing. It will be the most unuuuuusual field trip any class has ever been on. Come along, come along."

The class tramped onto a yellow bus parked in front of the school. As soon as the bus started to roll, they began singing a rousing chorus of "One Hundred Bottles of Beer on the Wall."

By the time the bus pulled into the parking lot of a small airport they were singing, "One bottle of beer on the wall, one bottle of beeeeer!"

Mrs. Gross stood by the bus driver. Giddy with excitement, she announced, "All right, stooodents. Hee hee! We're here. Step right down. Let's get moooooving! Just wait until you see our big surprise. It's beoooootiful! Just you wait, stooodents. Any questions? Good. Now come off the bus."

The surprise certainly was big. At the far end of the runway sat a giant silver blimp like the ones you might see hovering over football stadiums. The great shiny watermelon swayed in the breeze. Sunlight danced along its metallic sides. Attached to the underside was a long cabin that looked much like a modern trailer home. Thick cables tethered the whole thing to the ground.

Mrs. Gross led the line of students across the airport runway to the jumbo craft. She stopped at the foot of metal stairs that reached up to the cabin door.

"Now guess what, stooodents," she said. "We're going for a ride. Yeeeees, we are. We're going for a ride in this beoooootiful airship. Isn't that exciting? Sure beats a field trip to a stuffy art museum or a boring fire station, doesn't it? Come along. Right this way, stooodents. Right up these stairs!"

Bradley and Duncan climbed the stairs together. "And you said Mrs. Gross was a crabby teacher," Duncan said. "Well, what crabby teacher would take a class on a neat blimp ride?"

Bradley said nothing. His eyes were fixed upon the name painted above the cabin doorway:

He took a seat next to his friend. "I don't like this, Dunc," he said. "Something is not right about this field trip."

But Duncan wasn't listening. He was too busy pushing buttons on his armrest and making his cushy chair lean back and forward again.

At the front of the blimp sat a woman who appeared to be the pilot. "So! Everyone aboard, Miss Eraser?" she said. "It took me twenty minutes to fly here this morning. So! With the wind at our back we should be there in much less time." Bradley recognized the voice. It belonged to the lady with purple ankles.

A low hum filled the cabin as the blimp rose off the runway. Out the window Bradley watched the ground fall away and the yellow bus in the parking lot grow smaller and smaller until it looked like a little toy.

The scene turned to slate gray when the airship entered a layer of clouds. As the hum of the engine rose to a high whine, the blimp seemed to pick up a remarkable amount of speed.

Mrs. Gross walked down the aisle serving apple pie, apple tarts, and apple cider on a silver tray. "Here you are, stooodents," she said in her new cheerful manner. "Here are snacks that are goooood for you. Eat. Eat. An apple a day keeps the doctor from pay, don't they say? Now lower the seatback trays in front of you and eat up. Isn't this exciting? Isn't this fun? Everyone take something. Apples for everyone. An apple a day makes the doctor gray. So eat as much as you like. Hee hee!"

Bradley ignored the food. He sat staring into the swirling world outside the window. His stomach heaved as the blimp started to descend.

"Now guess what, stooodents?" Mrs. Gross called out. "We're going to land somewhere special. We're going to get off the blimp and take a walk. Has everyone had plenty of apple snacks to eat? Good."

Pedagog II emerged from the cloud cover. Now Bradley saw they were flying low over the ocean. With a shudder he peered forward and saw where the blimp was about to land—at the end of a peanut-shaped island. On the horizon, its tiered sides rising into the clouds like a colossal wedding cake, stood a white mountain.

"Chalk Mountain," Bradley said, remembering the map in the Teachers' Lounge. "And that's Apple Island down below. We're about to land on an island inhabited only by . . . only by teachers!"

Apple Island

The cabin door swung open. The metal stairs unfolded to the ground.

"Stooodents!" Mrs. Gross barked. "Exit the airship at once. Form a straight line at the bottom of the stairs." The jolly tone was gone from her voice. The scowl had returned to her face.

One by one the members of Bradley's class left the blimp and clumped down the stairs. They lined up silently along a white chalk line outside.

Bradley stood at the end of the line. The blimp, he noticed, had landed in the middle of a field, a soccer field. At either end stood a wooden goal. A weather-worn scoreboard read NORTHERN TEACHERS VS. SOUTHERN TEACHERS.

Clang! Clang! Clang! Mrs. Gross stomped down the metal steps followed by the lady with purple ankles. Silver whistles hung around both women's necks. With hands clasped behind their bottoms, they strode to the head of the line.

The purple-ankle lady addressed the class. "So! My name is Mrs. Gold Star. I'm Head Teacher of this island. I better not hear any snickering about my name. No! And I better not hear any talking in line whatsoever."

Bradley raised his hand. "Where are we?" he asked. "What are we doing here?"

Mrs. Gross sneered at the boy. "I told you we were going on a field trip, didn't I?" she said. "Well, we are in a field, aren't we?"

"And I better not hear any more questions," said Mrs. Gold Star. "So! Follow us!"

The two teachers led the students across the soccer field. They came to the start of a road paved entirely with speckled tiles. Nailed to an apple tree at the side of the road was a large cork bulletin board. Attached to the tree across from it were a round gray bell and an intercom speaker.

"Reminds me of the hallway in our school," Duncan said in surprise.

Mrs. Gross spun around. She squinted down the line until her eyes fell on Duncan. Few Halloween masks have been as fearful as the look on her face right then. "What did I say?" she howled. "Do you have eraser crumbs for brains? I said no more talking! That's the last time I will warn any of you sniveling nosedrippings! Understand? And do not even think of breaking any more ruuuules while you are here."

The class went stiff and silent. In a straight single file, they stepped onto the road.

Bradley stared forward. As he passed the bulletin board he read some letters cut from red construction paper thumbtacked to the cork:

GREAT HALL WAY Mile 0

Below this was a notice written on notebook paper:

RULES
No running
No pushing
No spitting
No loud voices
No cuts in line
No saving places
No chewing gum
No rollerblading
No skateboarding
No ball bouncing
No jumping rope
No hopscotch

Sneakers squeak-squeak-squeaked on the speckled tiles as the class walked along. The Great Hall Way cut a straight path through a forest of apple trees. Leafy branches reached far out, dangling shiny red apples above the children's heads. Every fifty steps or so, they passed a red alarm box with the words IN CASE OF FIRE, BREAK GLASS. They also passed white porcelain drinking fountains, but no one dared get out of line for a drink of water, nor did anyone dare visit the little cabins marked BOYS and GIRLS.

Now and then a blue bug with wiggly antennae and long back legs leaped onto the road.

"Cootie! Cootie!" the creatures chirped.

One landed near Bradley's feet, and—stomp!—he quickly put an end to it.

He overheard Mrs. Gross say at the front of the line, "Those pests are getting worse here up north, Head Teacher. Soon this whole island will have the cooties."

"I'll order Mr. Janitor to bring the cootie-catcher to this area immediately," said Mrs. Gold Star. "Now let's hurry. The bus is waiting."

A second cootie leaped toward Bradley, chirping, "Cootie! Cootie!" until he flattened it like the other. "So we're heading for another bus," he told himself. "I've got to ditch these teachers soon."

Fortunately, at school Bradley had a great deal of practice in escaping from lines. He knew that teachers rarely checked what happened in line behind them. So, as the head of the line disappeared around a sharp turn, he slowed his pace.

He counted to three and dove, landing in a pile of leaves behind a large apple tree. On his stomach, he froze and listened. Hearing no whistle blow, he peered around the tree trunk. "So long, teachers," he said. And with mixed feelings of bravery and fear, he watched his class continue up the road without him.

Bradley rose to his feet. "Now what?" he asked himself. "I need some sort of plan."

Nailed to the tree was another cork bulletin board. He read the notice thumbtacked on it:

GRAND PLAYGROUND 4 Miles
OFFICE PALACE 7 Miles
BIG BOOK BUILDING 10 Miles
TEACHER CITY 12.5 Miles

"Office Palace," he said. "I remember seeing that on the Teachers' Lounge map. It's at the foot of Chalk Mountain.

That's where I should go to get some information."

At that moment he heard footsteps and ducked back behind the tree. Around the corner marched two straight lines of teachers, mostly women, a few men. Some wore backpacks similar to the one he wore to school. One woman wore a cardboard crown that said BIRTHDAY GIRL on it. Two men carried lunchboxes. They all had ankles stained purple.

"This road could be crawling with more teachers, so I'll cut cross-country," he told himself. "As long as I can find that white mountain, I can find Office Palace."

Looking up at the bright sun overhead, he got his bearings and headed into the apple woods. The hiking was pleasant. The air smelled floral and polished like a classroom on a crisp Monday morning. Beneath the apple trees, soft grass that looked and felt curiously like green crepe paper blanketed the ground. Here and there yellow daffodils sprouted. When Bradley knelt to inspect one, he discovered something remarkable. The flower was made of yellow tissue paper, just like the flowers he had made last spring in Miss Purdy's class.

Stretched among the branches of a nearby apple tree was a curious-looking spiderweb. Long, flat strands, clear and sticky to the touch, formed the web. Dangling from it by another sticky strip was a peculiar plaid spider who moved up and down by reeling the strand in and out of its bottom.

"Scotch tape!" Bradley declared. "And I always thought Scotch tape was made in factories."

After hopping over a small brook flowing with a purple fluid that looked like pen ink, Bradley watched a snail the size and color of a dirty softball crawl through the crepe paper grass. The trail of cream-colored slime it left behind quickly hardened, and when Bradley pulled up a length of this material he found he was holding nothing less than fresh masking tape.

With the next step he slipped on squishy fallen apples. His knee smacked something hard and box-shaped that grew on a pedestal like a toadstool. When he saw the lid with latches he realized what this plant was—a lunchbox. Turning in circles, he found more of these lunchbox mushrooms growing around him.

Overhead flapped a flock of extraordinary birds. Blue, red, yellow, and green, they seemed to be made of folded paper in a variety of colors.

"Origami birds!" Bradley called out.

For several minutes he watched the birds flitter to and from an apple tree, building a nest out of pipe cleaners. Even the melody the birds chirped was familiar to Bradley, and he sang along:

Good morning to you! Good morning to you!
We're all in our places, with bright smiling faces.
Good morning to you!

Bradley walked on. Soon he entered a large clearing. A low wooden fence encircled acres of fresh green clover. Standing inside the enclosure, munching on clover, flicking their tails, and contentedly swaying back and forth, were dozens of white cows and an equal number of brown ones.

Bradley crouched behind an apple tree, on the lookout for teachers. Sure enough, two of them wearing yellow overalls crouched among the cows. Each wore a straw hat. Each had a plastic box filled with small cardboard cartons by her

side. One teacher, squatting beneath a white cow, held out a carton and pulled the cow's tail. The cow let out a low moan that sounded like "A-E-I-O-Uuuuuuu" as white milk squirted into the carton. When the carton was filled the teacher closed its peaked top and started filling another.

Meanwhile, the second teacher knelt beneath a brown cow. She also held out a carton. To Bradley's great surprise this cow squirted chocolate milk. "A-E-I-O-Uuuuuuu," the cow lowed. "A-E-I-O-Uuuuuuuu."

"So this is where our school cafeteria's white and chocolate milk comes from," he told himself. "And those are the half-pint cartons that are impossible to open and even more impossible to drink from without having milk dribble down your chin."

From his hiding place he heard the teacher under the white cow say, "Work, work, work! Day after day, eight-thirty to three o'clock, all we do is work. It's not fair. It seems as if recess was hours ago. I hate filling these cartons over and over and over. Boooooring! Tomorrow I'm going to play hooky and call in a substitute. How long until lunch?"

"Miss Bulletin Board, stop your bellyaching," said the teacher under the brown cow. "First you had a drink of water. Then you went to the bathroom. Then you complained that your stomach hurt and you needed to sit down. You ride the cows constantly and chat with any teacher who passes. We'll never get our job done if you don't stop fooling around."

Bradley had heard enough. He moved on.

TeacherVille

Skirting the edges of the cow pasture, careful to stay hidden from the two teachers, Bradley continued south.

Not far from the dairy he came upon a wrinkled cardboard sign written in black marker pen.

TEACHERVILLE .5 Mile

A narrow lane took him into a shady glen. There he discovered the remains of an abandoned village. Square white houses lined both sides of the lane. With their flat roofs caved in and large side windows smashed, the houses must have been vacant for many years. On almost every wall someone had spray-painted graffiti:

Bradley approached a house with a large "4" stenciled on the door. When he swiped his hand along the front wall, it came away smeared with white smudges.

"Chalk!" he said. "These houses were built with bricks of white chalk."

A cloud of dust rose from the floor as Bradley opened the door. The dusty furniture inside—a long table, four desks with chairs attached, four beds, and a sofa—stood in straight rows facing a wall painted black. A battered bulletin board, smashed fluorescent lights, fallen acoustic ceiling tiles, and dozens of ripped paperback books littered the floor.

"Open House. Tonight. Eight O'Clock," he read off a sign on the wall. But someone had scrawled CANCELED across it. Bradley left the house. He headed for the largest building on the lane. It had GYM written above the door. All at once a bell tolled from somewhere far south. Looking up the road, he spotted five woman teachers marching in single file toward him.

Again his four-square reflexes came into action. He sprang across the lane and dove behind the gym building just as the teachers walked past.

"I thought that Chalk Mountain bell would never ring!" one teacher shouted. "Lunchtime at last!"

"Hey, no cuts in line!" said a second.

"Dibs on the coffee pot," announced another.

"Stop pushing in back!" yelled the fourth.

Bradley watched the teachers file into a long building marked TEACHERS' CAFETERIA.

The village fell silent for a minute, then—Burp! Burp! Burp!—a sound matching the fire alarm at Bradley's school blasted from a speaker overhead.

The alarm repeated until the voice of Mrs. Gold Star blared out. "Attention, all teachers! This is not a drill. No! This is a real emergency. So! Make sure you are listening. There has been an escape. One of the juveniles brought to the island today has sneaked away. His name is Bradley! I repeat, Bradley Zimmerman! A boy . . . short . . . with carrot-colored hair that needs a good combing . . . wearing a white jacket and a shirt that's probably untucked. If you approach him, use extreme caution. He is sneaky and asks a lot of questions. The teacher who finds Bradley will earn an hour of free play on the Grand Playground!"

Even before the announcement ended, the front door of the cafeteria flew open and a dozen teachers burst into the street.

"I'll find him first," shouted one teacher.

"Hey, no cuts! No cuts!" shouted a second.

"Dibs on the little creep!" cried another.

"Here, Bradley! Here, boy! Heeeeere, Bradley, Bradley!" called a fourth.

In no time teachers were darting up and down the lane, shoving, tackling, and tripping one another.

Bradley raked his fingers through his hair and scrambled to his feet. He flew down an alleyway and across a parking lot. Ahead was a wide ditch. He leaped, made it, and tore into the woods.

The cries of the teachers followed him through the trees.

"Here, Bradley! Here, boy!"

"We have some cupcakes for you, young man!"

"Olly-olly-in-free, Bradley!"

"Braaaaaaaaaaaadley!"

Without looking back, Bradley ran for his life. He came to a hill and raced up its steep slope. Although the teachers' calls grew fainter and fainter, not until he reached the summit did he bend over to catch his breath.

Crossing the Grand Playground

Bradley faced south. At the bottom of the hill stood a chain-link fence running from east to west. Beyond the fence lay something he could never have imagined. Stretching out to the horizon was an expanse of blacktop decorated with white lines and circles.

"It's colossal! It's humongous! It's huuuuuge!" he said. "It's . . . it's the biggest playground in the universe!"

As far as he could see, countless climbing structures, handball walls, basketball hoops, slides, swings, sand pits, monkey bars, baseball diamonds, tetherball poles, volleyball nets, and every other imaginable piece of playground apparatus rose from the asphalt.

"With those teachers on my tail I can't stay here, and there's no going back," Bradley told himself. "Walking around that fence would take hours. I have no choice. I've got to go straight across that playground."

Bradley charged down the hill. When he reached the chain-link fence he crouched low. With still no teachers in sight, he sprang up. The fence rattled as he scrambled to the top. He swung his legs over and dropped, landing in a squat on the asphalt.

Again Bradley checked for teachers. A tall one with a whistle around her neck stood about fifty yards away. At once he dove out of sight behind a handball wall.

"That teacher looks as if she's on playground duty," he muttered. "I sure hope she's as out to lunch as the teachers on our playground who are supposed to watch us."

Bradley peered around the edge of the wall. Plenty of poles, walls, and climbing bars stood in his path to hide behind. But there were also plenty of teachers, running, chasing, swinging, sliding, playing hopscotch, and jumping rope. A dozen of them were playing Red Rover just beyond the wall.

Pweeeeeeeeeeeeeeeeeeeeeet!

The guard teacher had blown her whistle and Bradley froze with terror. "Miss Flash Card, stop chasing Mr. Report Card!" she bellowed. "One more time and you will be sitting on the bench for the rest of recess."

Bradley blew his breath out. Now was the time to make his move. He darted out from behind the wall and sprinted behind a tire swing. He slithered under a merry-go-round and sprang past a spiral slide, seconds before a teacher came zipping down it.

Now where? To the right was a softball diamond, to the left a sand pit. He raced across a basketball court and dove headfirst into the sand.

For another half-mile Bradley dodged from pole to pole, wall to wall, swing to swing, avoiding the notice of teachers who were everywhere, bouncing red balls, kicking yellow balls, swatting blue tetherballs, and smashing white volleyballs.

He stopped to catch his breath behind a baseball backstop. Ahead stood something colossal, something so wide and tall that it took him a moment to realize what it was—a giant jungle gym. This great matrix of iron poles, cross bars, and ladders reached up for hundreds of feet like scaffolding on the side of the world's tallest skyscraper.

Far, far above, Bradley saw tiny teachers clambering up, down, over, and across the metal bars like so many monkeys in the treetops.

"Doesn't look good," he said. "If one of those teachers looks down while I'm walking underneath this thing, I'm sunk."

Shadows of the crisscrossing bars slipped over Bradley as he headed southward beneath the jumbo jungle gym. All

went well until, dead ahead, two teachers swung down from the lowest bar. At once he wrapped his arms and legs around the closest pole and shinnied up. Grabbing a cross bar, he dangled in midair as the teachers strolled by just two feet beneath his sneakers.

"Crossing this playground is harder than hiding out in the Boys' Room during math," Bradley said. "Probably safer to travel above ground."

He climbed up twenty more levels. Step-slide-step-slide. He moved along the metal bar. Step-slide-step-slide. His head swiveled in all directions, alert for teachers. Step-slide-step-slide until he reached the end.

Bradley peered downward. The fastest way to the asphalt was by means of a slide that sloped in a wavy silver ribbon to a spot far, far in the distance. He sat at the top of the slide. He inched forward, pushed himself off . . .

Andheslidallthewaydownonhisbottom.

But now came the most perilous part of Bradley's journey across the playground. From the bottom of the slide he could see the chain-link fence that marked the southern boundary. But it lay beyond an open field with no place to hide. Even worse, a group of teachers was playing freeze tag in that field.

"You're It!" one teacher shouted.

"You missed me!" shouted another.

"Did not!" shouted the first.

"Did so!"

Bradley crouched like a runner in the Olympics, his eyes fixed on that fence. "This will have to be the fastest sprint of my life," he said. "At school if a teacher caught me running away, I'd only be sent to the principal's office. Here if I'm caught I hate to think what those crabby teachers might do."

As the tag-playing teachers tripped to the far end of the field, Bradley said, "Ready! Get set! Go!" and took off. But even before he ran ten yards—Pweeeeeeeeeeeeeeeeeeet!—a whistle blew and teachers from all over the place started shouting.

"There he is! There's Bradley!"

"Get him! Get him!"

"Trounce him! Bounce him!"

Bradley ran without looking back. From behind came the screech of whistles and screams from an angry mob of teachers.

He reached the fence dripping with sweat. In one swift motion he leaped and scrambled over the top. As he dropped down into tall weeds on the far side he glanced over his shoulder.

Twenty seething, scowling, squinting teachers stood in a row, rattling the fence with clenched fists. "We'll get you yet, Bradley!" they called. "Just you wait! You'll never get off this island!"

Back at school Bradley would have been elated to have run away from so many teachers. But here he was terrified.

The Teacher's Pet

The sun blazed straight overhead. The territory Bradley had entered was hot, dry, and barren. Boulders of white chalk studded the terrain. As he walked, Bradley kicked up puffs of chalk dust that coated his jeans and jacket. He might as well have been on the surface of the moon.

On the horizon, gleaming in the sunlight, stood Chalk Mountain. But it was still miles away.

Bradley removed his coat. "This desert is getting hotter and drier," he said. "If I don't get water soon I'll never make it to Office Palace."

Scrubby bushes bearing black, brick-shaped pods sprouted among the chalk boulders. Bradley inspected a pod on one bush closely, running his thumb over its flat, soft side. "An eraser!" he said. "Chalk erasers are growing on every bush around here."

Bradley walked for a while longer before brushing his arm against the spiky limb of a cactuslike plant. On closer look he made a second discovery. Each spike was a silver thumbtack.

The scorching sun beat down on Bradley as he staggered south. Gusts of wind whipped swirls of chalk dust into his face and hair. His eyes stung. His throat was parched.

"I'm so thirsty I have no spit left," he said as another blast of dust powdered his nose. "I haven't been this thirsty since the cracker-eating contest during lunch last week."

Fifteen minutes later he reached a high ridge. He trudged to the top and found himself overlooking the Great Hall Way. He ducked low as three teachers on bicycles whirred past on the speckled-tile road. Lying on his belly cowboy style, he studied the roadside. Next to a red fire alarm he spotted what he was looking for—a white porcelain drinking fountain.

He rose to his knees. He was about to charge down the hill when a loud squeal from behind made him jolt.

"Hey! Hey! I'm telling on you, Bradley. Hee! Hee! I'm telling!" said a voice. "Teachers won't like this one bit. Hi! Hi-i-i! You're in big trouble now. Ho! Hooooo!"

Bradley whirled around. There, squatting on a chalk boulder, was a creature about the size of a school desk. Yellow scales covered its entire body. Its long neck stretched toward Bradley, and its ugly face wore a grin that showed fierce teeth and a quick tongue.

Where had Bradley seen a creature like this before? After a second of thought he remembered—in volume G of the encyclopedia back in his school library.

"A gargoyle," he said. "You're a talking, moving gargoyle!"

The creature held a golden apple in its claws, constantly polishing it against its yellow belly. "Hey! Hey!" it repeated. "The teachers are looking for you, Bradley. Hee! Hee! And I found you. Won't they be pleased? Hi! Hi-i-i! You're in for it now, boy. Ho! Ho! Hooooo!"

Bradley brushed off his dust-caked shirt. "What are you talking about?" he asked. "What sort of creature are you exactly?"

The scaly creature swished its spiked tail, stirring up a small dust tornado that twirled off behind it. "Hey! Hey! Teachers like us, they do," it said. "Hee! Hee! That's why they call us teacher's pets. Hi! Hi! That's what I am. A teacher's pet. And when I wag my tattletale it means I'm going to tell on you, Bradley. And you're going to get it. Ho! Hooooo!"

"A teacher's pet?" said Bradley. "I should have figured there were some here too." He paused to study the creature before him. "So tell me, teacher's pet, why give me away? What's in it for you?"

The beast continued to polish the apple until it was as glossy as a mirror. "Oh, marvelous things, Bradley. Hee! Hee!" it replied. "The teachers might let me help change the bulletin boards. Hey! Hey! Or they might let me sit next to their desks while they grade papers. Hi! Hi-i-i! Or they might even give me another treat like this gorgeous apple I got for filling their coffee cups. Ho! Ho! Hooooo!"

As the beast talked, Bradley was thinking. How was he going to stop this creature from squealing on him? How did he handle teacher's pets before? Easy. Whenever Errol, the teacher's pet in his class, was about to tell on him, Bradley made Errol's life miserable until he swore to keep his mouth shut. Hiding Errol's headgear for his braces or filling his glue bottle with water was usually enough to keep him quiet.

The teacher's pet stretched its neck out farther. "I must go now, Bradley. Hee! Hee!" it said. "I'll find a teacher on the Great Hall Way and tell them where you are. Hey! Hey! Oh, won't they be proud of me! Hi! Hi-i-i! Aren't I wonderful? Ho! Hooooo!"

The creature raised its apple again to admire its reflection, and as it did so Bradley snatched it out of its claws. He held it above his head and said, "What a fine apple this is. I think it would be fun to throw it down to the road and watch it smash to pieces."

The teacher's pet slipped off the rock and slunk to the ground. "Hee! Hee, Bradley! You wouldn't do that, would you? Hoo! Hoo! Give me back my apple. OK? Hey! Hey!"

"Listen, snitch, and listen good," said Bradley. "You won't get back this shiny golden apple if you tell on me. Understand?"

"Oh, sure, Bradley. Hi! Hi-i-i! You're the boss. Whatever you want. Ho! Hooooo! You're my pal, my chum, my best friend."

Bradley pointed away from the road. "Then, old buddy, you better start heading that way right now," he said. And he tossed the apple as far as he could in that direction.

"Oh, thank you, thank you, Bradley. Hee! Hee! You're the best! Hey! Hey!" And with its spiked tail between its legs, the beast scampered off into the desert.

Bradley shook his head. "Pitiful," he said. "Teacher's pets. Their bark is always worse than their bite."

He was certain that the teacher's pet would not give him any more trouble.

Mr. Janitor

Spying no teachers on the Great Hall Way, Bradley charged downhill. Within seconds he reached the drinking fountain and turned the silver handle. Ahhh! Out gushed a high, arching stream of cool, clear water. He slurped and gulped, slurped and gulped. He splashed the water across his dusty face and let the water flow through his hair. He was lapping up some more when a sound—ch! ch! ch! ch!—came from down the road.

Bradley looked up. "Sounds as if someone is sweeping," he said.

He hid behind a thumbtack cactus and waited. Sure enough, around the bend appeared a man pushing an extremely wide broom. A cloud of dust rose from the speckled tiles as he walked, whistling a cheerful song. He wore blue overalls with an amazing number of pockets. A scrub-brush mustache wiggled under his nose while he whistled, and strands of gray hair hung like a damp mop from beneath a baseball cap.

When the man reached the fountain, he took a sponge from a back pocket and wiped the porcelain basin. He yanked a wrench from a side pocket and tightened a bolt

on the fountain handle. Next, he pulled a can of bug spray from a hip pocket and attacked the ants crawling around the fountain's base. Here he froze. He was inspecting the fresh sneaker prints in the dirt.

The man stood, drew a blue bandanna from a chest pocket, and wiped his brow. In a whisper he called, "Bradley. Hey, Brad, you around here?"

Bradley ducked down farther.

"Listen, if you can hear me, Brad, I have news for you. I was just mopping the cafeteria in Teacherville and heard the teachers talking. They're organizing a huge search party for you. It's like a great big game of hide-and-seek, and they're experts at it. Listen, you're in a fix, my friend, and I think I can help you."

From his hiding place Bradley studied the man. He didn't look like a teacher and he certainly didn't sound or act like a teacher. Maybe he should trust him.

When Bradley emerged from behind the bush, a grin spread across the man's tanned face. He pulled a feather duster from a back pocket and ran it over Bradley's dust-covered jeans.

"Looks like you've been through some rough territory, Brad," he said. "The name's Mr. Janitor. And it's an honor to meet you. You must be one clever kid, to have gotten this far across the island without being captured."

Bradley smiled. "Pleased to meet you, sir," he said. "I bet you do the cleaning up and maintenance work on the island."

"Like I said, Brad, you're one smart apple," said the man. "Yep, it's my job to keep this island running, all right. I'm the one who fixes anything that breaks. I clean up all the spills the teachers make. I shovel snow in the winter and wash the windows in the spring. I turn on the heat in the buildings each morning and scrub graffiti from the walls. And if a teacher gets sick, guess who cleans up the mess?

Me. I guess you can say it's my job to polish this whole Apple Island."

Bradley stepped behind the thumbtack cactus again as a line of teachers appeared around the corner.

Mr. Janitor removed weed clippers from a leg pocket and began snipping the crabgrass along the side of the road. "Good day, miss. Hello, sir," he called out as the teachers tromped by.

"The sink in the Girls' Room is clogged," one teacher called back.

"The blackboard in my house needs cleaning," said another.

"And there are cooties, cooties everywhere," complained a third.

When they were out of sight, Mr. Janitor said, "All's clear, Brad. As you could hear, those teachers can be crabbier than you could imagine. Real rotten apples. I think it's the crab apples they eat that makes them that way. But when you're shipwrecked on their island, you do what they tell you to do."

"Shipwrecked?" said Bradley. "You mean you're a castaway?"

"For twenty-five years," said Mr. Janitor. "You see, Brad, when I was young I was a crab fisherman. I had the prettiest crabbing boat on the Atlantic seaboard. Her name was Pulito. My, how I loved that boat! I spent hours painting her and scrubbing her, keeping everything shipshape and in perfect repair.

"One day I was far offshore in Pulito when I netted the most colossal crab in creation. I'm telling you, Brad, this crab was as big as a school bus and the same yellow color as one too. So, you see, instead of my pulling that crab into

my boat, the crab started pulling Pulito and me. Still caught in my net, he walked right along the ocean floor for miles and miles, hour after hour. And I couldn't let that crab go, Brad. Oh, no. I was determined to tire it out, haul it in, and have clam chowder for dinner.

"Finally after a week of being tugged by the giant crustacean, my dear Pulito hit some rocks off this island and sank. There I was, a mile from shore and not a good swimmer. I would have drowned, Brad, if that crab hadn't come to the surface, now free of my net, and grabbed me in its claws. I swear, Brad, that creature carried me right to this island and dropped me on the beach, where the teachers found me."

"And did they put you right to work?" asked Bradley.

"I only get a break when the teachers hibernate for two weeks around Christmas," said Mr. Janitor. "And that's how it's been all these years. But now tell me, Brad, how'd you get to this island? And what are you doing this far inland?"

"My teacher brought my class here on a blimp," Bradley explained. "I escaped, and now I'm going to Office Palace to find out why we're here."

Mr. Janitor nodded. He removed a knife from a back pocket and began scraping gum off a tile in the road. "I saw the Apple Island Express Bus come by this way a few hours ago, Brad," he said. "It was filled with boys and girls your age. Don't know where it was heading, but Office Palace might be the place for some information. Can't tell you for sure, though. I've never had a reason to go inside myself. But I do know that teachers guard the entrance day and night."

Bradley thought for a moment. If this janitor was anything like the janitor at his school, he knew much more about this island than any teacher did. "I bet you know a way into Office Palace without the teacher seeing me," he said.

Mr. Janitor grinned again. "You're a real shiner, Brad. Listen, this island has miles of tunnels running under it. Teachers used to mine down there. One of the abandoned mines runs right under Office Palace."

"Will you take me there?" asked Bradley.

"Don't see why not. There's an entrance to the mines a stone's throw from here."

After taking another drink of water from the fountain, Bradley followed Mr. Janitor into the brush. The man drew a small sickle from a hip pocket and whacked a path through the spiky thumbtack plants.

Soon they came to a wooden door in the ground.

"Here's the place," Mr. Janitor said. "Below this door are the great mines of Apple Island."

The Mines

Mr. Janitor fished through a front pocket of his overalls and pulled out an impressive ring of keys. He sifted through large brass keys, jagged steel keys, skinny bike keys, and rusty skeleton keys until he held up a small silver key and inserted it into the lock on the door in the ground.

Bradley helped pull the door open.

A warm blast of air buffeted his face as he peered down the mine shaft. A metal ladder dropped into inky blackness. Mr. Janitor stepped on the top rung. "Listen, Brad, there's a maze of tunnels down there," he said. "It's easy to get lost."

"I'll be right behind you," Bradley assured him. As Mr. Janitor's baseball cap disappeared underground, Bradley started down the ladder himself.

At the bottom he stood in warm, steamy darkness.

"It smells like the inside of my desk down here," he said. From some far-off place his words repeated in a low echo.

Mr. Janitor struck a match, and a burst of flames lit his face. He pulled a candle from a side pocket and lit it. The candlelight fell upon a dazzling collection of colors— lemon yellow, violet red, robin's egg blue, peach, carnation pink—that covered the smooth, glossy walls, ceiling, and floor of the tunnel.

Bradley ran his hand along one slick wall. "This mine is carved through crayon wax," he said.

Mr. Janitor held the candle up to the ceiling, and drops of green-yellow wax splattered on the floor. "Long ago a teacher named Miss Crayon discovered you could color pictures with this stuff," he explained. "The teachers used little hollow drills to bore out millions of sticks of it. Sixty-four colors in all they mined down here."

Holding his candle before him, Mr. Janitor led Bradley through the mottled tunnel, past layers of turquoise blue, veins of burnt brown, a bed of red-orange, and a large deposit of forest green. The passage sloped and rose, twisting to the left, then to the right. Flickers of light shot down dozens of mine shafts leading off to the sides.

Farther on, Bradley noticed pointy pink stalactites hanging from the ceiling and shiny gray stalagmites jutting up from the floor. He ran his hand over one stalagmite and examined his darkened fingertips.

Mr. Janitor removed a hammer from his pocket and broke off a chunk of a hanging stalactite. He handed the pink, rubbery piece to Bradley. "Two teachers named Mr. Lead and Miss Eraser hauled tons of these rocks out of the mines," he said. "They had invented a gizmo called a pencil and for years argued about how to make it. Miss Eraser was in favor of sticking her rubbery rock on the end of the wooden stick, not inside it. Mr. Lead insisted that his gray rock should go on the end. I forget who won."

"Miss Eraser did," said Bradley. "She's my teacher, and she always wins."

After two more turns the tunnel widened into a vast, dank chamber. Climbing the walls of this room was a tremendous tangle of rusty pipes, hissing tanks, spitting valves, spinning gears, rattling gauges, dripping faucets, and revolving wheels the size of pizzas. Plumes of steam shot from several pipes. The entire works seemed to be under tremendous pressure.

Twenty or so of the widest pipes extended across the cavern floor. Their ends dipped into small pools of bubbling liquid in a rainbow of colors and as thick as pancake batter. Mr. Janitor's candlelight fell upon a blue pool, a red pool, and a yellow pool.

Bradley recognized the smell from Friday afternoon art class. "Those pools are full of paint," he said.

Mr. Janitor removed duct tape from a back pocket and fixed a leaky pipe. "Right you are, Brad," he said. "I call this room the core of Apple Island. We're now directly under Chalk Mountain."

Bradley looked upward. The network of pipes and valves ran up the walls, disappearing into the darkness high overhead. Far, far above him, so high he had to squint to make out what it was, Bradley saw the smallest pinpoint of daylight.

"There are vast reservoirs of paint under the island," Mr. Janitor explained. "A teacher named Mrs. Science had the idea of using the steam pressure from these pools to generate electricity. This room powers the entire island."

Mr. Janitor led Bradley past more bubbling pools of paint—a purple one, an orange one, a green one—and down another tunnel.

Long, mosslike plants grew in the cracks in the cavern walls. Bradley figured out at once that the plants were paint brushes. He pulled one out and dipped it into a pool of brown paint. BRADLEY WAS HERE, he painted on a wall.

After a mile the tunnel ended. Another mine shaft with a metal ladder attached led upward.

"Here's where I leave you, Brad," Mr. Janitor said. "This ladder leads into Office Palace. I must get back to my sweeping before the teachers notice I'm absent."

Bradley stepped onto the ladder and started to climb. Halfway up, he heard Mr. Janitor call after him. "Listen, Brad, one word of warning. If you go into the southern half of the island, don't eat the apples. They're crab apples."

Office Palace

When Bradley reached the top of the ladder, he pushed open the trap door. Soon he found himself standing in a brightly lit room with white walls. He faced a chart with a big E on top. Surrounding him were a tall scale, a full-length mirror, a bed, and a sink with a hot-water bottle draped over it. STOP, DROP, AND ROLL read a sign above a shelf that held all sorts of plastic pill vials, Band-aids, and bottles of calamine lotion. The place smelled of rubbing alcohol and throw-up.

"A first-aid room," Bradley told himself. "Just like the one next to our school office."

Turning toward the mirror, he hardly recognized the boy with dusty red hair, pencil lead smudges on his cheeks, and thumbtack scratches on his chin. He opened the door an inch and peered into a long, wide hallway. Good, no teachers in sight. He opened the door wider and stepped into the hall.

Squeak! Squeak! Squeak! went his sneakers on the polished floor. Overhead, crystal chandeliers hung from a vaulted ceiling spangled with golden stars. Portraits of teachers lined the walls. On one side of the hall, Bradley spotted Mrs. Gross's picture, her frightening scowl and all. On the opposite wall hung a painting of the kind Miss Purdy. The portrait hanging next to Miss Purdy's was also familiar. But where had he seen that teacher before? The bronze plate underneath it read W. T. MELON.

As Bradley continued down the hall, he read aloud the words stenciled on the doors. "Supply Room . . . Copy Machine Room . . . Resource Room . . . Thinking Hat Closet . . . Lost and Found Room." But only one room caught his interest enough to make him stop. "Torture Chamber," he said. "This I have to check out."

He pushed through the door. Expecting to find the instruments of torture he had seen only in books—racks, thumbscrews, maybe a cat-o'-nine-tails—he found items that were much more familiar. In a corner stood a stool with a conical dunce cap sitting on it. One wall held a blackboard on which someone had written, over and over:

I will not waste time.
I will not waste time.
I will not waste time.
I will not waste time.

Bradley found hickory sticks and rulers and wooden paddles and a dark closet with a small chair in it and a small desk with a sign taped to its hard surface: PLACE HEAD HERE.

"This is a torture chamber," he said. "A classroom torture chamber with all the punishments in classroom history." After a quick glance at a bench along the back wall he rushed from the room.

At the end of the hall, Bradley faced a tall glass door. Taped to it was a notice printed in purple ink:

ALL VISITORS SIGN IN PLEASE

He pulled open the door and stepped up to a counter. The countertop being a foot above his head, he stood on a stool to see over it. There he spotted an extremely pretty

woman tapping rapidly on a computer keyboard. He cleared his throat, hoping to be noticed.

The woman, without looking away from her computer screen, said, "Sign in, please."

Bradley opened a spiral notebook on the countertop. The list of visitors who had signed the book was impressive:

Christopher Columbus
Ferdinand Magellan
Capt. John Smith
Francis Drake
Bluebeard the Pirate
Amelia Earhart
Santa Claus
Charles Lindbergh
Crew of the Space Shuttle Discovery

All at once a voice spoke over the intercom on the woman's desk. "Miss Secretary? Send this memo to all teachers: There will be no more food fights in the Teachers' Cafeteria. I repeat, no more food fights."

"Yes, Your Highness," replied the woman.

Bradley signed his name in the notebook and cleared his throat once more.

Again the woman talked without looking up. "Name, please?"

"Bradley," said Bradley.

"Well, Mr. Bradley, if you have come to use the phone, make it quick. If you have lost something, the Lost and Found is down the hall. If you have found something, ditto. If you feel ill, go to the First-Aid Room at once."

Before Bradley could say a thing, the intercom interrupted again. "Miss Secretary? Send this memo to all teachers: There will be no more kicking red balls on the Grand Playground. I repeat, no more kicking red balls."

"Right away, Your Majesty," said the woman.

"Excuse me, madam," said Bradley. "I'd like to see the person in charge."

"So you were sent here, Mr. Bradley," said Miss Secretary, continuing to work. "What did you do wrong? Chew gum on the Great Hall Way? Take cuts at a drinking fountain? Throw a stink bomb into the Girls' Room?"

"No, no," said Bradley. "I wasn't sent here at all. I came to see the person in charge. Is there a principal in this office?"

The woman raised her thin, curved eyebrows. "You mean Prince Apple?" she said. "He does the ruling around here. But no teacher ever wants to see His Excellency."

"But I'm not a teacher. I'm a boy!"

Finally Miss Secretary stopped her keyboard tapping and looked toward the counter. Her brown eyes widened and her red lips spread wide. "Oh, my! You're right! Oh, you're a miracle! You are a boy!" she said.

Bradley turned apple red. He had never been called a

miracle before. "I'm nine years old but tall for my age," he said.

"How marvelous! How amazing! You're the first boy I've seen in years and years. Where did you come from? Were you shipwrecked? Did a tornado bring you here? I had no idea any children were on this island. Oh, how dull this place has been without them!"

"But the teachers brought my entire class here," said Bradley.

The woman's eyes widened even farther. "I must tell the prince at once," she said. She leaned over and spoke into her intercom. "Sire, you won't believe this, but there's someone here who wants to see you. And he is not a teacher. He's a boy!"

"A boy? A boy who wants to see me?" came the reply. "Why, this is a historic day! Send him into the throne room at once."

Miss Secretary again smiled at Bradley. "Right through those doors," she said. "Prince Apple will be happy to see you."

Prince Apple

The wide doors behind Miss Secretary's desk swung open. Redder than ever, Bradley slipped past the woman and stepped into the next room.

The throne room was small and cramped. The walls were lined with filing cabinets, a tilting stack of papers standing on top of each one. Red, yellow, and orange light filtered through an apple-shaped stained-glass window, flooding the floor and a large wooden desk in the center of the room with color. Above the desk a large pendulum swung slowly back and forth, back and forth. Behind the desk, almost hidden by more stacks of paper, sat a small man in a swivel chair. He wore a white shirt and a long tie decorated with apples—yellow ones and red ones. On his head sat a brown, bucket-shaped crown that could have been easily mistaken for an overturned wastebasket. He swiveled in his chair one way and then the other, watching a plaid spider climb the far wall.

Bradley stepped nervously toward the desk along a red carpet. "Prince Apple?" he said.

The man spun toward him and smiled. Bradley had seen smiles similar to this one on his principal's face and

knew it could mean anything.

"Ahhh!" said the man. "Hmmm!"

Bradley swallowed. "You're the ruler of this island?"

"Uh-huh," said the man, nodding.

"Well, sir, my name is Bradley, Bradley Zimmerman, and I was wondering if you could help me."

"Aha!" said the prince, raising a finger.

Bradley shuffled his feet and continued. "You see, sir, my teacher, Mrs. Gross or Miss Eraser as you call her, brought my class to this island on a blimp."

"Huh?" went the prince. He leaned toward his intercom and spoke loudly. "Miss Secretary, send this memo to all teachers: There will be no more classes brought to Apple Island on a blimp. I repeat, no more blimp rides for classes."

"But, you see, sir, I escaped from the teachers, and I walked all the way to Office Palace."

"Ahhh!" said the prince, nodding.

"But now I don't know what to do!" said Bradley. "I think my class is in danger. It all has to do with something called Operation Misteach."

"Uh-oh!" said Prince Apple, returning to the intercom. "Miss Secretary, another memo, please. To all teachers: Anything called Operation Misteach will end immediately. I repeat, Operation Misteach is canceled."

Bradley was beginning to have a bad feeling about this visit. "You see, sir, I thought you might know what the teachers were planning," he said. "Would you know where they took my class?"

The prince shook his head slowly. "Uh-uh," he said.

"So you don't know what is happening on this island?"

"Uh-uh."

"You don't know anything about Operation Misteach?"

Prince Apple drummed his fingers on the desktop. "Well, uh, the fact is, Bradley . . . ," he said. "Um, I haven't been out of Office Palace for a long, long time."

Bradley let out a long sigh. "So you're a prisoner on this island, just like Mr. Janitor."

"Uh-huh," said the prince. "The teachers used to find me useful. They let me make up rules, handle the discipline, that sort of thing. I also made sure the Supply Room was well stocked with freshly picked thumbtacks and crayons from the mines. But that was many, many years ago."

"So what do you do all day besides send out memos?" asked Bradley.

"Ugh, evaluations," said Prince Apple. "I write reports on the teachers and give each of them a yearly grade."

"But how can you grade teachers if you never leave Office Palace?"

"The Head Teacher tells me what grade to give," said the prince. "Teachers who do exactly what all the other teachers do get good grades. The teachers who do anything different get a poor grade. Once a teacher tried reading a book—poor grade. Once a teacher asked to leave this island because she wondered what was beyond the horizon—very poor grade."

"But isn't that what teachers tell us kids to do, read books and wonder what the world is like?"

"Hmm," said Prince Apple. "You ask too many questions, Bradley. I'll give you the grade D-."

Bradley pointed to the ceiling. "So what's that swinging thing for?" he asked.

The ruler of Apple Island waved his hand above his head. "That's the Great Pendulum of Education," he explained. "It's a reminder that teachers should never allow education to move forward. If it moves forward one year, it must move backward the next. Forward, backward. Forward, backward."

"You mean like in my school. One year they taught reading one way and the next year it was a completely different way and now they're teaching it the way they did before."

"The Pendulum of Education must keep swinging," said Prince Apple. "Even though the three R's—reading, writing, and arithmetic—have changed little in centuries, teachers must constantly change how to teach them."

"Sounds like teachers are more confused than the kids," said Bradley. "I don't even know why they call them the three R's when only one of them starts with R."

"Uhhh, like I said, Bradley, you ask too many questions," said Prince Apple.

Bradley now realized that his long trip to Office Palace had been a waste of time. "But if you can't help me," he asked, "how am I ever going to find my class?"

"Hmm," said Prince Apple, pulling his chin for a moment. Then he spun 360 degrees in his chair and said, "Aha! I remember a place where you can go to get some information. Try the Big Book Building, three miles down the Great Hall Way. I heard it's filled to the rafters with books. At one time it contained every book ever written in every language in the world."

"I guess that's where I should go," said Bradley. "Sorry to leave so soon, sir, but I have a class to save." And he turned and ran toward the door.

Prince Apple pointed his finger at the boy's feet. "Uh, Bradley?" he called out. "There's a rule against running in Office Palace."

"Sorry," said Bradley. And he walked out the door.

Purple Lake

As Bradley left the throne room Miss Secretary looked up from her computer screen with a smile. "Are you really going to save your entire class?" she asked. Apparently she had listened on her intercom to Bradley's conversation with Prince Apple.

Bradley grew crimson again and shrugged. "Guess so," he said. "I'll try my best."

"That's so brave," said the woman. "I doubt many boys would attempt such a daring rescue."

"It's nothing," said Bradley, shrugging some more. "Nothing at all."

He stumbled toward a door marked EMERGENCY EXIT and pressed the metal bar. With a clang the door opened and he was out of there.

Outside the exit stood two teachers with silver whistles around their necks. Quickly Bradley ducked behind a long hedge. Bending low, keeping his ear cocked for the sound of a whistle, he followed the hedge to the corner of Office Palace. The Great Hall Way now lay only twenty yards away. After checking in both directions, he sprinted across the road and leaped into the brush.

The land Bradley had entered was dank, damp, dense, and difficult to walk through. The trees grew so close together their branches allowed only gray sunlight to reach the ground.

Bradley inspected the hard yellow fruit dangling from the gnarly limbs. "Crab apples," he said. "I must be in the southern half of Apple Island."

The tree branches clawed at Bradley's pants and shirt as he trudged on. Thick moss, identical to the green felt in his classroom, covered the twisted trunks, and a chilly, coffee-colored fog clung to the swampy ground. Squish! Squish! Squish! went his sneakers in the soft red muck that looked and smelled like modeling clay.

After a mile or so Bradley entered a narrow ravine. Steep walls, as smooth and black as chalkboards, rose on both sides of him.

"Hope I don't meet any teachers in here," he said. "I'd be trapped."

SHHHHHHHHHHHH!

Bradley froze. The sound had come from somewhere ahead. "Who's there?" he called.

SHHHHHHHHHHHH!

"Must be the wind," he said.

SHHHHHHHHHHHHH!

Bradley decided to experiment. He clapped his hands.

SHHHHHHHHHHHHH!

"It's some kind of echo," he said. "Maybe this is where teachers came up with that sound to quiet kids."

SHHHHHHHHHHHHH!

"Hey! I'm Bradleeeeeey!" he shouted.

SHHHHHHHHHHHHH!

"And teachers can't stop me!"

SHHHHHHHHHHHHH!

Shortly after leaving the ravine, Bradley arrived on the sandy shores of a large lake. He would have enjoyed a quick swim except that the liquid in the lake was dark purple. Small purple waves lapped up on the white sand.

On the beach lay three teacher's pets, sunning themselves.

"Hey! Hey! Hee! Hee! Hi! Hi-i-i-i! Ho! Hooooo!"

Bradley approached the water's edge, shaking his fists. "Get lost! Scram! Get outta here!" he shouted, and the scaly yellow creatures scampered into the brush.

Crouching, Bradley stuck a finger into the lake's purple fluid. "This entire lake is filled with ink!" he said. "I'd better be careful. My mom would kill me if I got a spot on this shirt."

Clear hollow reeds grew in the shallows. They gave Bradley an idea. He broke off one reed and dunked it into the lake. He was holding something that looked remarkably like a pen.

"Now if only I had something to write on," he said.

He turned toward a grove of trees behind the beach. The leaves on these trees were white like paper and rectangular like paper. They were smooth like paper and fluttered in the breeze as paper would do. Bradley reached up and felt one leaf. "This is paper," he said. Then on it, with his newly crafted pen, he wrote BRADLEY WAS HERE in his best cursive handwriting. At that moment Bradley heard chattering and ducked behind a tree. Up the beach two teachers were strolling toward him. Each teacher carried two wooden buckets. While one picked paper leaves off a tree, the other removed her shoes and waded into the lake.

"You know, Miss Paper," called the wading teacher, "isn't it your turn this week to collect this writing solution? I hate putting my feet in this blankety-blank stuff."

"Remember, Miss Ink," replied the other, "we all take turns doing duties on this island."

"Yes, but ever since those goody-goody teachers left, we have twice the number of jobs to do."

"You've been bellyaching about that for over one hundred years, Miss Ink. Now just do your work, and make it snappy. We must get back to S.C.H.O.O.L. The assembly begins in two hours."

From his hiding place Bradley looked on. "So that explains why all the crabby teachers have purple ankles," he told himself. "They've all been wading in this inky lake."

Miss Ink dipped her pail into a dark wave. "Wasn't it great fun this morning making that typical class write those blankety-blank stories?" she said. "I must say it was excellent practice for us crabby teachers."

"Yes, teaching writing is quite simple," said Miss Paper, continuing to pick leaves. "You just order a class to write a story, then for the next hour you can sit at your desk and drink coffee."

"But I hate wasting those leaves on story writing," said Miss Ink. "They're much more useful for making paper airplanes and spit wads and cootie-catchers."

Miss Paper's buckets were now full. "You know, Operation Misteach is going exceedingly well," she said. "After these training sessions many more of us can go to America. We should have every school there under crabby teacher control by June."

Miss Ink waded to shore with her buckets. "And next school year we can begin misteaching in Europe and Asia and Africa and everywhere. Soon we'll be doing that blankety-blank teaching all over this blankety-blank-blank planet."

As the two teachers strolled back up the beach they sang a little song:

> *Misteach! Misteach!*
> *The best way to preach.*
> *Why instruct right when you can*
> *Misteach! Misteach!*

Bradley leaned against the tree trunk. "This Operation Misteach is bigger than I thought," he said to himself. "Not only do I have to save my class, but I have to save my whole school. And not just my school, but all the schools in the world!"

Bradley was more convinced than ever that the Big Book Building was the best place to go. He took off southward in a run.

Meeting Miss Library

A long and tiring trek, through more crab apple woods and more modeling clay swamps, brought Bradley to an enormous red-brick building. A giant stone apple sat on each side of a broad stairway. The stairs led up to tall

wooden doors, and chiseled in stone above the doors were the words:

APPLE ISLAND BIG BOOK BUILDING

Bradley's eyes grew wide. "Imagine the number of books this humongous place must hold," he said, bounding up the stairs.

He pulled the doors open. Inside the building the light was dim, and the place smelled of mold. Bradley had to fight his way through streams of cobwebs to reach a check-out counter that was covered with an inch of dust.

Next to the counter sat a cardboard box with a sign:

RETURN BOOKS HERE

Bradley picked up a book from the box and read the title: *How to Cook Turkey*.

"Who would check out a book like this?" he said, remembering to use his soft library voice.

Checking the card on the inside pocket, he read, "Pilgrim Mothers and Fathers. Due: November 1620."

He picked up a second book, *How to Fly Kites*. The checkout card read: "Ben Franklin. Due: October 1774." A third book, called *How to Grow a Garden*, had been checked out by Mary Mary. Due: February 1860.

Bradley looked from one far end of the building to the

other. "All these people found the information they need-ed in this place," he said. "But how am I ever going to find a book that will help me?"

Behind the counter parallel rows of book stacks, far too many to count, rose to the high ceiling. The aisles between the shelves stretched outward, ending in a small dot far off in the distance.

Few things excited Bradley more than a room full of books, especially one this size. He strolled down an aisle, reading the titles on the leather book spines and forgetting where he was or why he had come there. Here and there he pulled down a volume and thumbed through it, always remembering to replace it in its proper spot. So engrossed was he in the books that he failed to notice the long and lumpy form lying in his path. He stumbled over it, then looked back and with a shudder realized what it was—a

body. It was the body of an elderly woman with an open book on her lap.

For a long moment Bradley scarcely breathed. To his relief the woman finally stirred.

"I'm sorry. Excuse me. My apologies. I beg your pardon, ma'am," he said.

She was a white-haired woman who wore spectacles so thick that Bradley had a hard time telling if her eyes were open or shut. She sat up, rubbing her eyeballs behind the thick frames. A thin smile, like a crack in a walnut, spread across her wrinkled face.

"Howdy, there," the woman said. "Must have dozed off. And you must be Bradley. I've heard your name mentioned twenty times over the loudspeaker today. Welcome to my Big Book Building, brave boy. My name is Miss Library. How can I help you? What are you looking for?"

"Friends, ma'am," said Bradley.

"Books on friends are in the 360 section," said the woman. "That's two rows to your right, then down seven tenths of a mile."

"No, no, I mean I'm looking for the place where my friends might be," said Bradley.

"Geography books are in the 910s, twelve aisles over, three tenths of a mile down on your left."

"No, Miss Library, my friends are on this island," Bradley explained. "I think they are in a place called S.C.H.O.O.L."

A look of disappointment crossed the woman's face. She

looked over her glasses at the boy and shook her head. "Sorry I can't help you there, Bradley. I don't know much about this island. I don't know anything about what's happening outside these walls except what I hear on the intercom and read in these books."

Bradley sat on the wooden floor by the woman's side. "So the teachers are keeping you prisoner too!" he said. "Just like Prince Apple and Mr. Janitor. How did you end up on Apple Island, Miss Library?"

The woman leaned against the bookshelf. "Mercy. Although it happened so very long ago, I can remember every detail," she said. "It happened when I was ten years old. A young lady who loved to read. Not just books, though. I loved reading every word on anything I saw— magazines, newspapers, cereal boxes, street signs, can labels, milk cartons, candy wrappers, even the labels inside my shirts and dresses.

"I lived in London, England, at the time, and on that terrible day I was sitting in Kensington Park. I was reading the entire C volume of my encyclopedia. The sky was so sunny and I was so immersed in my book that I never noticed who dropped a golden apple in the grass by my side. But there it was and there I was, so I picked it up and put it my book bag.

"No sooner had I done this than I spied a second golden apple only yards away. I picked this treasure up as well, only to find a third one and a fourth a little farther on. In this manner I soon filled my book bag with golden apples as I stepped farther and farther into a meadow of tall crabgrass. I found the last apple behind a crab apple tree. As I bent to pick it up everything turned brown. Someone had thrown a burlap bag over me. Arms wrapped around my legs, and more arms wrapped around my shoulders. Like a sack of potatoes I was dumped into a car. With only my ears as a guide, I knew I was being driven to a sea harbor and taken onto a boat. After many hours in that stuffy bag I finally fell asleep. When I awoke I was sitting in this building. The teachers put me to work at once shelving books, and I've been here in the Big Book Building ever since."

Bradley looked down the long row of books. "But besides shelving books, what do you do in here all day?" he asked.

"I read," the woman answered. "I start at the end of one row and read through the books to the other end, sleeping wherever I end up each night. I can tell you everything about philosophy, psychology, economy, astronomy, chemistry, botany, zoology, and technology, but since I haven't reached the geography books yet, I know little about Apple Island."

Bradley blew on a book and a puff of dust rose in the air. "Sad this building isn't used more," he said.

"I heard that at one time the Big Book Building was the busiest place on this island, always filled with curious teachers reading and finding information," said Miss

Library. "Not anymore. I still find a few black and white bookworms slithering from stack to stack, but the crabby teachers never come in here. They keep writing books, though, for me to shelve. They're full of opinions and stories about themselves, but no one actually reads what they write."

Bradley rose to his feet. "It's been nice chatting with you, ma'am, but now I have to rush. I'm on a mission. I came here to find out what happened on this island."

"History books are thirty rows over and half a mile down," said Miss Library. "I'll take you there on the motor-ladder."

For the first time Bradley noticed a tall stepladder behind the woman. The ladder stood on wheels and had a motor attached between its legs. He climbed to the fifth step while Miss Library stood on the lowest. She fiddled with some dials and said, "I'm setting the controls to take us right to the section we want, Bradley. Hold on tight. This ladder can rip."

The motor hummed softly. Miss Library shouted, "Blast off!" and the ladder shot down the aisle at a spectacular speed. Near the checkout counter the contraption tilted on two wheels and careened around a corner. It rocked wildly side to side as it rolled along the front of the stacks.

Miss Library waved her arms like a cheerleader. "Rock and roll!" she cried. "Yahooooooo! Faster! Faster!"

With a screech of wheels, the ladder took another sharp

turn. Rattling and clattering it tore down the aisle and skidded to a halt by a sign reading TEACHER HISTORY 990.

"Voilà!" said Miss Library. "Here we are. But I do need to oil those wheels. The ladder's moving much too slowly nowadays."

Bradley forced his white fingers to let go of the ladder's sides. Miss Library scanned the lower bookshelves as he checked the upper ones, reading the titles aloud. *How I Spent My Summer Vacation* . . . *The History of History* . . . *The Most Horrid Homework Ever Assigned* . . . *The Blackboard Is Always Greener in the Next Classroom* . . . No, I see nothing up here that could help."

"But there are lots of books on Apple Island down here," said Miss Library. "Take your pick."

Bradley stepped down from the motorladder. From the lowest shelf he pulled out a thick book bound in red leather. ·

"This book should tell me what I want to know," he said. "It's called *The Truth About Teachers*, and it was written by Prince Apple."

The Truth About Teachers

Bradley and Miss Library sat side by side on the floor of the Big Book Building. Bradley opened the cover of *The Truth About Teachers*. The first page was familiar. It showed the Apple Island map that hung in the Teachers' Lounge back at school.

He flipped the page and began reading aloud.

All teachers, every single one of them, come from an island located far out in the Atlantic Ocean. It is named Apple Island. The island is divided in two halves. In the South, hard, sour crab apples grow. That is where the crabby teachers reside. Most of them live in the large, noisy urban sprawl, Teacher City. The North has pleasant pastures and forests of apple trees bearing delicious red apples. The kind teachers once lived in this part of the island, on farms and in the tidy village of Teacherville.

Bradley lowered the book. "I haven't seen a friendly teacher all day," he said. "And Teacherville is in ruins."

"Go on, go on," said Miss Library. "I wonder what happened."

Bradley turned the page. "Chapter Two might explain things. It's called 'The Squabble.'" He continued to read.

For centuries the entire race of teachers lived together in peace on Apple Island. Whenever an argument arose, I, Prince Apple, would solve it with my expert conflict-management skills.

No one knows how the squabble started or who was to blame, but it began during the annual tag tournament on the Grand Playground. Some teachers say the fight started when a teacher named Mr. Jump Rope from the South tripped Miss Recess from the North. Mr. Jump Rope said it was an accident, that he didn't mean it, that if Miss Recess didn't have such big feet she wouldn't have tripped in the first place. But Miss Recess insisted he tripped her on purpose. One thing led to another until every teacher from the North was arguing with every teacher from the South. The Grand Playground became an ugly scene of name-calling, shouting, pinching, pushing, scratching, and sticking out tongues. The bickering became so bad that the island was on the verge of a full-scale civil war.

"My turn. My turn to read," said Miss Library, and Bradley handed her the book. She pushed back her glasses and continued the story.

Five days of squabbling passed before the one thousand teachers who lived in the North held a meeting in the

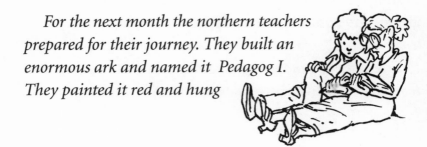

Teacherville Gym. A teacher named Miss Lost-and-Found stood before the group and said, "Those southern teachers are getting crabbier and crabbier all the time. This island is no longer safe for us. It is time to leave."

Next a teacher named Miss Globe addressed the meeting. "I was in the Big Book Building yesterday and read about a land called America. It has spacious skies, amber waves of grain, and purple mountains from sea to shining sea. It sounds like a beautiful place to go."

"I make a motion that we build an ark to carry us to this place called America," called out Mr. Woodwork.

"All in favor of abandoning Apple Island to get away from the crabby teachers, raise your hand," said Miss Assignment. One thousand and one hands went up, including the two raised by Mr. Class Clown, who sat in the back.

"So the kind teachers left the island, leaving the crabby ones behind," said Bradley.

Miss Library thumbed through the book, scanning the pages as she went. "Well, listen to this," she said.

For the next month the northern teachers prepared for their journey. They built an enormous ark and named it Pedagog I. They painted it red and hung a brass bell from the rafters of its peaked roof. The kind teachers loaded Pedagog I with bags of red apples, blocks of chalk, boxes of crayons, baskets of pencils, barrels of ink, bales of paper, bins of books, and all the other supplies they would need in the new land.

In the month of September they sailed from Apple Island. The journey was brutal. Fierce storms battered the good ship Pedagog I for nine months. Finally, one day in mid-June, the teacher on lookout blew her silver whistle and shouted, "I spy with my little eye . . . Land!" When the teachers reached shore they agreed to take a vacation. For the next three months they fished, swam, played baseball, and stayed up late at night.

Miss Library handed *The Truth About Teachers* back to Bradley. "The next chapter is called 'S.C.H.O.O.L,'" he said.

Upon arrival in America, the kind teachers discovered that many people lived there. Some of the citizens were tall like the teachers, but some were extremely short. These short people were called children.

In September, when the long vacation was over, the teachers held another meeting. First to speak was a lanky teacher named Mr. Tetherball Pole. "I find the small citizens interesting," he said. "They are fun and nosy and like to giggle. Too bad they don't know how to read books, write stories, or do math problems. I suggest we teach them how."

"Hear, hear!" called the others.

"We can build a large house where the small ones can come and learn each day," suggested Mrs. Bulletin Board. "We can call it the House Of Official Learning—H.O.O.L. for short."

"But we don't want any of those tall people to come," said Mrs. Scissors. "They are too boring. They're always rushing off to meetings and worrying about something called money. I want to teach only the small citizens. We should call our new learning house the Small Citizens' House Of Official Learning or S.C.H.O.O.L."

"All in favor of teaching in a place called S.C.H.O.O.L., raise your hand," said Miss Assignment. One thousand and one hands went up, including the two raised by Mr. Class Clown.

"My turn to read again," said Miss Library. She took the book and flipped through the pages, stopping at a chapter called "Teachers Today."

Although teachers enjoy teaching the small citizens, there is a good reason why they change classes each year. They do not want their students ever to discover a dark teacher secret. But I, Prince Apple, will tell it to you. Teachers never were young and never grow old. They always appear exactly the same as they did on the day you met them.

The kind teachers eventually built S.C.H.O.O.L.s all over the world. Unaccustomed to the manners and habits of the rest of the planet, however, they rarely venture off school grounds, day or night. If you are sneaky you might spy them *playing on the playgrounds late on moonlit nights. They'll be zipping down a slide or swinging on a swing to remind them of the carefree days back on Apple Island.*

Miss Library slowly closed the book. "What remarkable things you learn by reading," she said.

"But there are still some mysteries," said Bradley. "Like how come my teacher, Mrs. Gross, is teaching in my school? She's the crabbiest teacher in the world. And I still don't know why the crabby teachers brought my class to this island."

Miss Library stood and studied the bookshelf above her

head. "Voilà!" she said. She pulled out a yellow paperback called *The Truth About Teachers* (Revised Edition), written by Mrs. Gold Star, and she handed it to Bradley. He opened the book and discovered another map. This one showed only the southern half of Apple Island, including the enormous Teacher City. "With all the misteaching going on, I won't believe one word in this book," he said. "But there's no reason for this map to be incorrect." Examining the map, he found what he wanted. Southeast of the Big Book Building was a black, L-shaped figure marked S.C.H.O.O.L.

"That's where my class must be," he said.

"Good chance," said Miss Library. "There have been announcements on the intercom about a big assembly going on there this afternoon."

The two remounted the motorladder. "Blast off!" said Miss Library, and away they rolled.

By the time Bradley could catch his breath, the ladder had stopped before the checkout counter. He gave Miss Library the paperback and she stamped the card inside.

"This book will be due in one hundred years," she said. "Don't forget that it is your responsibility to get it back on time."

"Yes, ma'am," said Bradley. "But now I must hurry to S.C.H.O.O.L."

Miss Library gave Bradley a hearty pat on the shoulder. "Good luck on your quest, young man," she said. "You have quite a challenge ahead of you. But I believe with your courage and determination you will reach your goal. Adieu! Ciao! ¡Adiós! So long!"

Outside the Big Book Building, Bradley reopened *The Truth About Teachers* (Revised Edition). He studied the large L marked S.C.H.O.O.L. on the map.

"Miss Library is right," he said. "That building is not going to be easy to reach. It's smack in the middle of Teacher City."

Teacher City

Two miles southeast of the Big Book Building, Bradley climbed a small hill. From the summit he saw the tall red-brick skyscrapers of a bustling metropolis, Teacher City. He beheld a breathtaking panorama of lights and signs and yellow buses moving along a maze of streets, and hundreds

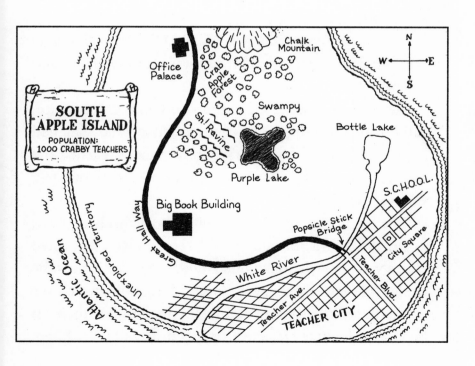

Chalk Mountain

Office Palace

Crab Apple Forest

Swampy

Bottle Lake

SOUTH APPLE ISLAND

POPULATION: 1000 CRABBY TEACHERS

Sh'l Ravine

Purple Lake

S.C.H.O.O.L.

Great Hall Way

Big Book Building

Popsicle Stick Bridge

City Square

Unexplored Territory

Atlantic Ocean

White River

Teacher Ave.

Teacher Blvd.

TEACHER CITY

N
W · E
S

of doll-size creatures crossing the streets that could be only one thing, crabby teachers.

But separating him from the great city was a wide river. It flowed with something white, thick, and very slow-moving.

Bradley climbed down to the riverbank. He stuck his finger into the white stuff. "Glue!" he exclaimed. "A whole river of glue!"

According to his map, Bradley stood on the banks of White River, which began to the north at Bottle Lake. Of course the river would be impossible to swim across, but downstream stood a bridge that took the Great Hall Way across into Teacher City.

"If I'm ever going to reach S.C.H.O.O.L.," he told himself, "I'll have to cross that bridge in plain view of all those teachers."

He starting hiking along the riverbank. Once, twice, three times he slipped on the hardened glue that had lapped up onto the shore. When he finally reached the speckled-tile road he crouched behind a wastebasket as a yellow bus zoomed by.

The bridge spanned the river a short distance away. From this point, Bradley could see it was constructed entirely of Popsicle sticks glued tightly together. Below the bridge a dozen teachers with long fishing poles were fishing in the white river. Apparently they had ridden there on bicycles, for a bike rack close by was nearly full.

"Just what I need!" Bradley said. He stole from his hiding place and lifted a bike from the rack. He checked the road both ways before climbing on, then pedaled like mad.

He reached the bridge in high gear. He didn't look back. He didn't look at the river of glue beneath him. His eyes remained fixed on a large bulletin board on the far side.

"If I can make it behind that thing, I'll be out of sight and safe," he said.

Up-down, up-down pumped his knees. Never had his

legs moved so fast. Luckily his gym teacher had been making him do lots of exercises during P.E.

When he was finally across the bridge he squeezed the hand brakes. He skidded to a stop behind the bulletin board and leaped off the bike. On his knees he peered around the cork to read the yellow cutout letters thumbtacked to it:

TEACHER CITY
Crab Apple Capital of the World

Below this a notice read:

Today's substitutes:
Mrs. Pen substituting for Mr. Pencil
Miss Glue substituting for Mrs. Paste
Mr. Marker substituting for Mrs. Crayon
Today's events:
10:00 Birthday party for Mr. Spanking Machine
12:00 Good-bye party for Miss Yearbook
2:00 Assembly at S.C.H.O.O.L.
Teecher of the day:
Miss Spelling

Before him lay the intersection of two busy roads, Teacher Boulevard and Teacher Avenue. The streets teemed with teachers. Teachers scurried in and out of the tall red-brick buildings. Teachers walked in straight rows along the sidewalks. Teachers filled the yellow buses that rattled up and down the streets, and teachers on bicycles wove between the buses.

Bradley read several billboards posted along Teacher Avenue:

READING IS NO FUN
WATCH THE VIDEO MADE FROM
THE BOOK INSTEAD

LEARNING TIMES TABLES IS STUPID
USE A CALCULATOR!

DON'T DO IT
TEACH IT

He pulled the paperback from his pocket and consulted the map again. "S.C.H.O.O.L. is fifteen blocks up Teacher Avenue," he said. "If I stay in the shadows of these tall buildings I bet I can make it all the way without being seen."

Bradley waited for a line of teachers to pass, then darted into the first doorway down the avenue.

This happened to be the doorway of the Teacher Toy Store. He paused long enough to admire the items in the display window—plastic counting blocks, number lines, abacuses, play clocks, ten rods, scales, and fake money. "All the stuff we use in math class," he said.

Keeping in the shadows, Bradley next dodged into the doorway of the Teacher Rhythm Instrument Market. He would have loved to mess around with the tambourines, triangles, cymbals, and drums displayed in this window, but he had to keep moving.

By ducking from doorway to doorway, past the Teacher Cupcake Bakery, Halloween/Valentine Party Supplies, Room Mothers Rental Agency, and the Field Trip Travel Agency, Bradley made his way down Teacher Avenue without being spotted by a single teacher.

At the corner stood a teacher wearing an orange vest. She held a stop sign attached to a stick. When she stepped into the yellow crosswalk, two buses came to a halt and a long string of teachers crossed the street in single file. Bradley waited for the traffic guard to turn her back before bolting across the road himself.

Now he stood in the doorway of the largest building on the street. A brass plaque on the wall read:

TEACHER CITY TEXTBOOK FACTORY

Curious, Bradley slipped into an alley by the side of the building. Through an open window he spotted crooked stacks of shiny new textbooks. Two teachers, a big-eared man in a black turtleneck and a sharp-nosed woman in a blue pantsuit, sat behind computer screens.

Putting his ear to the window Bradley heard the man say, "So how is your science book coming along, Miss Rubber Band?"

"Great fun, Mr. Fire Drill," the woman replied. "Operation Misteach has certainly made textbook writing more interesting. Get this—I'm writing a chapter about magnets. I'm telling those cuckoo-brained children that two magnets will attract only if they like each other. Har! Har! If they hate each other, they will repel. Isn't that a gas?"

"Yes sirree!" replied Mr. Fire Drill. "Today I'm rewriting

the social studies books, and I've thought up some whoppers. Did you know Greenland is named that because everything there is painted green? Did you know Iceland is one big skating rink? Yes sirree!"

"And tomorrow we rewrite the history books," said Miss Rubber Band. "Get this—Head Teacher has ordered us to write that she was the teacher who discovered America, and she invented the telephone, and she walked on the moon before any man did. Har! Har! Rewrite the past and you've rewritten the present, she told me."

Bradley had heard enough. He left the alley, muttering to himself.

Three blocks farther down Teacher Avenue, he stood on the edge of the town square. In the center of the square stood a gazebo where eight teachers sat playing plastic recorders.

"Hot Cross Buns," said Bradley, recognizing the tune.

Dozens of other teachers, picnicking on peanut butter sandwiches and cartons of milk, sat on the crabgrass enjoying the concert.

The only place Bradley could find to hide was inside a dumpster. He hoisted himself up and dropped inside. Flies buzzed around his head as he crouched on empty shoeboxes, wads of colored paper, egg cartons, toilet paper tubes, and old newspapers.

"How am I ever going to get across that park?" he asked himself.

He sat thinking until . . . Bang!

Bradley peered over the edge of the metal container. An empty yellow bus was rolling slowly down Teacher Avenue.

Bang! Bang!

The bus backfired again, and then, with a loud squeal of brakes, it stopped next to Bradley's dumpster.

With horror, he watched the front door of the bus fold open. In the driver's seat, squeezed in tightly behind the steering wheel, sat a large man. He wore an oil-stained T-shirt that shone almost as brightly as his bald black head.

The bus driver pointed a finger the size of a hot dog at the dumpster. The finger curled, beckoning Bradley to come into the bus.

"This is it," Bradley said to himself. "I'm in for it now."

S.C.H.O.O.L.

The musicians in the gazebo played "The Itsy-Bitsy Spider" on their recorders. Three origami birds tweeted along in the crab apple treetops. The teachers, spread out on the crabgrass, continued to picnic and chatter. But inside the dumpster Bradley sat frozen in fear.

Again the man in the yellow bus motioned to him. "Psst, young gentleman!" he called out. "I can see you in that dumpster. No hiding from me."

Bradley searched for a safe place to run to. But teachers filled the square in front of him, and teachers filled the sidewalk behind him.

"Come on, Bradley, step on it!" called the bus driver. "I'm no teacher. Now get on this bus."

Bradley decided to chance it. He climbed from the dumpster and leaped up the stairs of the bus. He slumped low in the front seat.

"Are you one of the Apple Island castaways?" he asked.

The large man pulled on a silver crank, and the door closed. "You got it, young gentleman," he said. "The name's Bus Driver . . . Mr. Bus Driver. I've been following the news of your escape on the bus radio all day. And I'm telling you, the teachers are steaming mad about that. I figured you might be headed for Teacher City, so I came looking for you."

"I need to find my class," said Bradley. "I need to save them from Operation Misteach."

Mr. Bus Driver turned the ignition key. Bang! The motor backfired, then roared. "It so happens I dropped off your class at S.C.H.O.O.L. this morning," the man said. "The teachers are up to something big. They've been packing into that place all afternoon. Not even when the teachers get ready to hibernate around Christmas have I seen them this excited. I'll take you to S.C.H.O.O.L. right away."

With a sputter, more bangs, and a grinding of gears the bus rattled down Teacher Avenue.

Sitting low in the seat, Bradley watched the driver's eyes in the rearview mirror. "How'd you end up on Apple Island, Mr. Bus Driver?" he asked.

The man smiled into the mirror. "It's a crazy story, young gentleman. But if you want to hear it, I have time to tell it. You see, when I was a boy my greatest passion was puttering with motors. I loved taking them apart and timing how fast I could put them back together. There wasn't a motor in the world I couldn't assemble blindfolded.

"When I got older I wanted to drive anything with a motor—cars, motorcycles, semis, fire engines, lawn mowers, tractors, dragsters, bulldozers, golf carts, power boats, you name it. I even became a pilot so I could fly airplanes, jets, and helicopters.

"But one night, while I was flying a small plane, this crazy thing happened. You see, the night was spectacular. Every star in the heavens was blinking, and every constel-

lation—the Big Dipper, Draco the Dragon, Orion the Hunter—appeared not as a group of stars but as a clear picture. I'm telling you, young gentleman, the Milky Way was as white as White River flowing with glue.

"Well, I was studying the constellation Cancer the Crab when all at once the entire constellation began to move. No fooling. That giant crab in the sky starting waving one of its claws at me. Needless to say, I was riveted. I couldn't take my eyes off the thing, and I steered my plane straight for it. For hours, mesmerized by that waving crab, I flew my plane out over the ocean. Finally the motor coughed and cut out. No more gas. Lucky for me, I spotted the twinkling lights of an island and managed to glide the plane toward it. It so happened that I landed on the Grand Playground of Apple Island.

"Crabby teachers holding flashlights suddenly surrounded my plane and tied me up with jump ropes. I've been their captive, driving the Apple Island Express Bus, ever since. To this day the remains of my plane serve as a climbing structure on their playground."

Just as he finished his story Mr. Bus Driver drove the yellow bus past a chain-link fence and a sign reading:

TEACHER CITY PUBLIC S.C.H.O.O.L.

Beyond the fence stood a beige, L-shaped building. The sight caused Bradley to sit up straight in his seat. The structure was a copy of his school—the same large windows, the same tall gym, the same flagpole out front, although the flag flying from this one was green with a large red apple and a small yellow apple in the middle.

Mr. Bus Driver ran a hand over his smooth head. "Now, young gentleman," he said, "how are you planning to get inside that building?"

"If this S.C.H.O.O.L. is the twin of my school, I know lots of ways to sneak in," Bradley said. "It comes in handy whenever I'm tardy."

Mr. Bus Driver parked the bus in front. He pulled on the door crank, and Bradley slipped from the bus. He ran to the side of the building, where he found the cafeteria kitchen door.

As he had hoped, the door opened when Bradley pulled on the handle. He quickly slipped inside the kitchen, past the serving counter, and into the cafeteria. He could have found his way there with his eyes shut. Apparently lunch had just ended, for messy spoons and half-filled bowls of applesauce still lay on the long tables.

Bradley eyed the leftovers. "I'm starving," he muttered. "But Mr. Janitor had good reason to warn me against eating southern apples."

Walking down the hallway, Bradley passed the office and the library, both vacant. He entered a classroom, a duplicate of his own, complete with five rows of desks, a green blackboard, and a metal teacher's desk. But why did every item have a label on it? A small sticker above the coat closet read COAT CLOSET, and a sticker on the bulletin board said BULLETIN BOARD. The pencil sharpener had a tag on it that said STUDENTS USE ONLY WITH PERMIS-

SION, and a squirt gun sitting on the teacher's desk had a label that read FORBIDDEN.

BRRRRRIIIIIIIIIIIIIIIIIIING!

After the bell rang, a voice boomed over a loudspeaker. "Attention, class! Form a straight line in the hallway. The assembly will begin in five minutes."

At once the classroom door across the hall opened, and out came Bradley's class, marching in single file. As if guided by some remote control they stood in a line so straight it could have been made with a ruler.

That's strange, thought Bradley. No one is talking. No one is shoving or taking cuts.

Spying no teachers, he called out, "Hey, Dunc! Hey, Errol! It's me, Bradley! What's happening?"

But no one turned. No one said a word.

"Hey, everybody," Bradley called out. "There's free ice

cream in the cafeteria!"

Still no one moved. Something was very wrong.

"Class, proceed to the gym!" ordered the voice on the loudspeaker.

On command the class marched toward the end of the hall.

Bradley cut in line behind Duncan. When none of his classmates protested, he told himself, "Something's wrong. Something's terribly wrong with my class. They're doing exactly what the teachers tell them to do."

The Assembly

Left, right, left, right. Bradley's class tramped into the gym. They passed rows and rows of metal folding chairs, each holding a teacher with purple ankles. All Bradley could do was to stay in line and copy whatever his classmates did. They stared forward, so he stared forward. They marched in unison, so he marched in unison. They stood as straight as yardsticks before the stage, and so did he.

Four teachers sat on the stage. One teacher holding a clipboard stood. She stepped behind a podium and spoke into a microphone. "Good afternoon, teachers."

The microphone squealed, causing the audience of teachers to giggle and make faces and cover their ears with their hands.

"My name is Miss Attendance," said the woman with the clipboard. "Say 'Here' when I call your name. Miss Arithmetic!"

"Here," piped a high voice in the middle of the gym.

During roll call, Bradley's belly was as tight as a spit wad. He prayed none of the teachers would notice his knees shaking or the drops of sweat running down his forehead. He scarcely breathed until Miss Attendance called, "Mr.

Zero!" and a teacher in back shouted, "Present!"

"Thank you, teachers," said Miss Attendance. "Everyone is here today."

Next, the second teacher on the stage stood. The gym erupted with wild applause, whistles, and hoots as she stepped behind the podium. Bradley recognized her at once—Mrs. Gold Star.

"Today is the conclusion of your training here at the Small Citizens' House Of Official Learning, otherwise known as S.C.H.O.O.L. So! From now on you will not be just teachers, but schoolteachers. Repeat that, please."

"Schoolteachers," the teachers chorused.

The Head Teacher pointed her ruler at Bradley's class. "Before you stands a typical class of juveniles," she said.

"We brought these specimens to our island so that you could practice giving a typical lesson during a typical day at a typical S.C.H.O.O.L., and you all performed typically."

There came more clapping and cheering from the crowd.

"However, these typical

children did not eat a typical lunch," said Mrs. Gold Star. "No! We served them our special crab applesauce. So! When they leave Apple Island in a few hours they will remember nothing. Tonight when these typical juveniles return home, their typical parents will ask them a typical question, 'What happened at school today?' And they will reply, 'Nothing,' which is a typical answer."

Another thunderous ovation filled the gym.

"So! Already Operation Misteach is under way. Already a small, select team of crabby teachers has joined real S.C.H.O.O.L.s in a place called America. Repeat that, please."

"America," chanted the teachers.

"Now it is your turn to leave Apple Island," said Mrs. Gold Star. "You will enter a real S.C.H.O.O.L. and begin teaching our mislessons! Soon every schoolchild will know what we want them to read. They will believe only what we want them to believe! Operation Misteach will give us power! Operation Misteach will give us control of all S.C.H.O.O.L.s! Operation Misteach will give us control over the entire world!"

This sent the army of teachers into a wild frenzy. They began banging on their metal seats, stomping their feet, whistling through fingers, and chanting, "Misteach! Misteach! Misteach! Misteach!"

The Head Teacher slapped her golden ruler on her palm. "Shhh! Quiet, everyone," she said. "Now, lady and man teachers, it's time to introduce our first guest instructor.

Here is a teacher we all know and adore. The inventor of the tests you will be giving in your new schools—spelling tests, multiplication tests, essay tests, achievement tests, etcetera. Repeat that, please."

"Spelling tests, multiplication tests, essay tests, achievement tests, etcetera," chanted the audience.

"Now here she is . . . Miss Exam!"

"Good afternoon, fellow teachers," said the short, bony teacher who stood at the podium. "I'm here to teach you how to give tests. First, you will be delighted to learn that children in S.C.H.O.O.L.s hate tests. After you teach your students from the Operation Misteach manual, drill and drill them on the ridiculous information you just fed them. When they're about to fall asleep, when the classroom is the most warm and stuffy, it's time to give them a long test. It's that simple."

"Bravo! Bravo!" shouted the teacher audience.

"Now a word about grading," Miss Exam continued. "Suppose after all the hard work you teachers have done lecturing and drilling, your students fail a test. Up to this point an F was the worst grade you could give them. That's not fair to us teachers. I suggest adding G, H, and I grades, and if they still don't do well on your tests, go right down the alphabet to Z. Thank you."

"Bravo! Bravo! Bravo!" cheered the teachers as Miss Exam sat down and Mrs. Gold Star returned to the podium.

"So!" said the Head Teacher. "Now here's a little test for

all you crabby teachers in the audience. I will ask a few questions about how important it is to treat the girls differently from the boys in your class. First question. What subjects should you expect boys always to do better in than girls?"

A forest of arms flew in the air. The teachers groaned and squealed. Some stood up to make their hands go higher.

"It's important to choose the highest hand and the hand of the student who makes the goofiest noise," said Mrs. Gold Star. "That is usually a boy, so I will call on Mr. Stapler. Mr. Stapler, in which subjects should you expect girls to do poorly?"

"Math and science," said the man teacher.

"Excellent," said Mrs. Gold Star. "Math and science. Repeat that, please."

"Math and science," said the teachers.

"And I hope these girl juveniles before us never get any bright ideas that they can become an astronaut or an engineer or a scientist. No! Those are jobs for men, who are much better in math and science," said Mrs. Gold Star. "So! Next question. What job would a boy be silly to consider when he grows up?"

The audience remained still and silent.

"No? Then I'll give you a hint," said Mrs. Gold Star. "This job is considered one of the most important jobs in the world. But only women have the gentleness and patience for it. Still no hands? Then I will tell you. You must make certain that boys in your class never consider becoming . . . ta-daaa . . . a kindergarten teacher."

"Hear, hear!" shouted the teachers, followed by a great round of giggles.

"And so!" said the Head Teacher. "I'd like to introduce our next speaker—the inventor of something else you should assign often in your new classrooms. Let me introduce to you . . . Mr. Homework!"

A tall man teacher stood and bowed. "There's a lot of Operation Misteach information we want schoolchildren to learn," he announced. "And we want them to learn it as fast as possible. I suggest you give your students at least five to six hours of extra work each night. Thank you."

Wild cheers! Hoots! Whistles! Banging of chairs!

Mrs. Gold Star waved her ruler again. "It is now time to present our annual Gold Star Award!" she called out. "I wish to present this year's award to a teacher who has done much to put Operation Misteach into action. What is more, she managed to bring her own class here today for us to practice on. Lady and man teachers, I wish to present the Gold Star Award to Miss Eraser!"

Miss Eraser, alias Mrs. Gross, suddenly appeared from behind a curtain. There came a smattering of applause as Bradley's teacher walked up to the podium. She pinched the hem of her dress and curtsied to the Head Teacher.

With great ceremony Mrs. Gold Star pinned a large gold star onto her chest.

"Thank youuuuu, Head Teacher. Thank youuuuu, fellow teachers out there," Mrs. Gross said, blowing kisses to the crowd. "Thank youuuuu especially to the six teachers I always needed in my work, Miss A, Miss E, Miss I, Miss O, Miss U, and sometimes Miss Y. I also wish to thank Mr. Verb, who kept me moving, and Mrs. Noun, the person, place, or thing who was most helpful to me. Thank youuuuuu to my lovely poooooodle, Natasha, and to my goldfish, Sparky."

"Thank you, Miss Eraser," the Head Teacher interrupted, and Bradley's teacher backed off the stage blowing more kisses.

"So! There you have it, teachers," said Mrs. Gold Star when the noise died down. "Your training is complete. It is time to spread Operation Misteach across America. Onward to conquer the schools! Onward to conquer the world!"

"Misteach! Misteach! Misteach! Misteach!" the teachers chanted. They hugged one another and patted one another on the back and did silly dances in the aisles.

"So! Class of juveniles!" bellowed the Head Teacher. "Go! Proceed back to the bus!"

Rescue

Bradley's class marched out of the gym in the same robot-like fashion in which they had entered. Bradley still could not breathe too deeply, blink too much, or make a single sound, for the teachers were following the line of students, dancing, laughing, and shouting, "S.C.H.O.O.L.'s out! S.C.H.O.O.L.'s out!"

While the students filed onto the bus, the teachers wrestled, swung backpacks, and turned cartwheels on the front lawn. Some recited a silly poem:

No more students; no more books.
No Head Teacher's dirty looks.

As he climbed the bus stairs, Bradley caught Mr. Bus Driver's wink and sat in the front seat. In the rearview mirror the driver mouthed the words "Where to?"

"Let's just get out of here," Bradley whispered. "I think some teachers plan on coming with us."

Mr. Bus Driver pulled the door crank and the door slammed shut. He turned the ignition key and floored the gas pedal. Bang! Bang! went the motor. The rear wheels spun on the gravel before the bus finally moved forward.

PWEEEEEEEEEEEEEEEEEEEEET!

Hundreds of teachers blew their whistles at once. The bus rattled past them and out of the parking lot.

At last Bradley let out a long breath. He turned to see an angry pack of teachers standing in front of the S.C.H.O.O.L. shaking their fists at the escaping bus.

The buildings of Teacher City swept by the bus windows in one red blur. Up Teacher Avenue the bus tore, past Teacher Boulevard and onto the Popsicle stick bridge. As it crossed over White River, Mr. Bus Driver called out, "What are we going to do?"

Bradley leaned forward. "What can we do against all those teachers?" he asked. "At school I sometimes trick one teacher at a time. But here there are a thousand after us."

Mr. Bus Driver looked at Bradley in the rearview mirror. "Listen, young gentleman," he said. "Against all odds you managed to cross this entire island alone. You found your class and rescued them from S.C.H.O.O.L. You certainly aren't the type of kid who gives up easily."

Bradley continued to stare out the window. Yes, he was proud of what he had managed to do today. Early that morning he never imagined he had such ability. Ability. Wasn't that the word Miss Purdy wrote on his report card last year?

Bradley has a lot of ability. However, he should apply

himself more to his schoolwork. Bradley needs a challenge. Someday he will do great things.

"Last year Miss Purdy believed in me," Bradley said to the window. "And here on Apple Island, Mr. Janitor, Miss Secretary, Miss Library, and Mr. Bus Driver never doubted that I could come this far. Maybe I can stop all those crabby teachers. Maybe I can stop Operation Misteach."

As the bus passed the Big Book Building, a plan blinked into Bradley's brain faster than a flashcard answer.

"Stop the bus!" he commanded. "Mr. Bus Driver, I am going to save the schools!"

The bus brakes squealed, and the bald driver pulled the door crank. Even before the bus had stopped, Bradley flew out the door. He bounded up the Big Book Building stairs three at a time.

Miss Library sat behind the dusty checkout counter reading.

"Come on, ma'am," he called to her. "I'm taking you out of here. We're leaving Apple Island."

The woman dropped her book in the return box. "Hallelujah!" she said. "I'm right with you, Bradley."

Miss Library squinted at the sunlight as Bradley led her out the front door and onto the bus.

"Step on it!" the boy cried.

Bang! Bang! The yellow bus rolled down the Great Hall Way, sputtering and backfiring. It rattled past Purple Lake and headed toward Chalk Mountain.

Outside Office Palace, Bradley repeated, "Stop the bus!"

He leaped off the bus again and sailed past the teacher guards. Act quickly and sometimes teachers won't have time to react—that was his motto back at school, and it was working here as well. He was inside Office Palace before the teachers touched their whistles.

"Come on, come on!" he called to Miss Secretary. "We're busting out of here. A bus is waiting outside."

"At last!" said the pretty woman.

Bradley burst into the throne room and came out dragging Prince Apple by the arm.

"We're leaving Apple Island, Your Highness," Bradley told him. "We're all going."

"Huh?" said Prince Apple. "Um . . . Uh . . . Rrrrrrrr."

His wastebasket crown clanged to the floor as Bradley pulled him out the door. Miss Secretary flipped off her computer and ran after them.

But no sooner was everyone back on the bus than the alarms posted up and down the speckled-tile road erupted with a tremendous Burp! Burp! Burp! "That's the general Apple Island alarm," said Mr. Bus Driver. "Soon every teacher on the island will be trying to stop us."

Sure enough, a mile farther down the Great Hall Way, a tall barricade of desks and chairs blocked the road. The bus squealed to a stop. Before the mound of furniture stood a mob of snarling, scowling, cursing, glaring, jeering, nostril-flaring, spitting, stomping, fist-shaking teachers.

"There's the little troublemaker!" one teacher shouted.

"I have first dibs on him!" called another.

"You're going to sit with your head down on a hard desk for the rest of your life!" threatened a third.

Bradley turned toward the bus passengers. "When teachers get this worked up, they're hard to outsmart," he said. "But I think I know a way out of this."

He whispered something into Prince Apple's ear. He pointed to Chalk Mountain close by and whispered some more.

The prince flipped his tie through his fingers. "Ohh!" he said. "Ahhhhh!"

Things were tense as the two climbed from the bus. Prince Apple ran off toward the mountain. The teachers ignored the man, just as they always had. Bradley stood alone as the fuming band of teachers swarmed around him. Step by step they closed in.

Bradley smiled and shrugged his shoulders. "I really didn't mean to get out of line back there on Great Hall Way," he said. "It was an accident. Honest. I'm sorry. I'm really sorry. I promise never to do it again. On my honor. Cross my heart, hope to die. It wasn't my fault. Why blame me? Someone made me do it. They dared me. Really. I didn't do it on purpose."

By now the teachers stood so close to Bradley that he could see hairs quivering in their noses. He smelled the coffee on their breath.

Then a miracle. From high atop Chalk Mountain a bell began to toll.

"Afternoon recess time," one teacher immediately called out.

"Oh goody," said another. "It seems a bit early, but I can sure use a coffee break."

"I have dibs on the new basketball," said a third teacher. "We'll deal with you later, Bradley. Stay right here. Don't do a thing until we get back."

Then every teacher at the barricade took off in the direction of the Grand Playground.

Bradley waved to the bus. "Come on, everybody," he said. "Recess is only ten minutes long. We must get this road cleared."

Mr. Bus Driver, Miss Secretary, and Miss Library piled out of the bus. They began tossing the desks and chairs to the side of the road. Soon Prince Apple joined them.

"What just happened?" asked Miss Library, pushing a swivel chair into a ditch.

"Bradley is a true genius," Prince Apple said. "He told me to pull the Chalk Mountain bell cord to make the teachers think it was recess time."

"I figured these crabby teachers would never pass up a coffee break," Bradley explained. "No matter what they were doing."

Back on the bus, Mr. Bus Driver revved up the motor and crushed the gas pedal. "Where to next?" he asked.

"We need to find Mr. Janitor," Bradley answered. "I think I know a way to stop those crabby teachers from doing any misteaching ever again."

Colorful Rain

Around the next bend, Mr. Bus Driver hit the brakes again. The yellow bus stopped a foot in front of Mr. Janitor, who was still sweeping the Great Hall Way with his wide broom. He calmly pulled a spray bottle and a sponge from his overalls and began wiping bugs off the bus windshield.

"Mr. Janitor!" Bradley called out. "We need your help."

"What's up, Brad?" the man asked.

"Where's the closest entrance to the mines? We must get to the boiler room under Chalk Mountain. I have a plan to get all of us off this island."

Mr. Janitor's scrub-brush mustache quivered. "And I bet you're just clever enough to do that, Brad," he said. "Follow me."

Mr. Janitor led Bradley through some thumbtack bushes to a door in the ground. He opened it with the silver key off his key ring and disappeared down the ladder. By lighting match after match he showed the way through the dark tunnels until the pair stood in the large chamber filled with pools of bubbling paint.

Bradley studied the steaming valves, hissing faucets, and dripping pipes. "We'll open everything up," he said. "We'll

let all the paint under Apple Island flow."

"But, Brad, that will cause this entire mountain to blow its top," said Mr. Janitor.

"Exactly," said Bradley. And he began spinning wheels, yanking levers, and turning knobs as if he were in a video arcade. "We're leaving this island, Mr. Janitor. We should be able to reach the blimp before things really get going."

Mr. Janitor pulled a large wrench from a side pocket. "Now I got you," he said, and began loosening every bolt in sight.

Within seconds the great tangle of pipes began to rattle. Seconds after that the floor, walls, and ceiling started to shake. A pencil lead stalagmite toppled over and broke to pieces. An eraser stalactite snapped off the ceiling and bounced dangerously around the floor. From somewhere deep underneath the island came a low rumble.

"Time to peel out of here," said Mr. Janitor. "This mountain is about to explode."

Bradley followed Mr. Janitor's shaking match flame back down the tunnel. By the time the two were back on the bus, the ground was quaking violently. Red paint oozed from the summit of Chalk Mountain like a skinned knee. It flowed in bloody stripes down its white sides.

"We must get to the blimp, Mr. Bus Driver," said Bradley. "I sure hope it's still parked at the end of the road."

No sooner had the bus begun to roll than—

PHOOOOOOOOOOOOOOOOOOOOOOMMMM!

—the mammoth mountain of chalk erupted.

Out the bus window, Bradley, Mr. Janitor, Prince Apple, Miss Secretary, and Miss Library witnessed a great geyser of red paint gushing straight up from the mountaintop.

"Ahhhhhhhhhh!" said Prince Apple.

"It's a miracle!" said Miss Secretary.

"Thar she blows!" shouted Miss Library.

"How do you like them apples, crab teachers?" said Mr. Janitor.

"Reminds me of the time I squeezed the ketchup bottle too hard in our school cafeteria," said Bradley.

As they watched, the jet of red paint turned orange, the orange turned yellow, and the yellow turned purple. Shortly afterward, colored rain began to fall. Heavy globs of paint—red, orange, yellow, and purple—splattered upon the ground and drummed upon the roof of the bus.

"Wow!" said Bradley. "Modern art."

"I sure am glad I don't have to clean up this mess," said Mr. Janitor.

Mr. Bus Driver shifted gears. "Hold on, everyone," he said. "The ride could get rough."

Bang! Bang! Slipping and sliding on the slick tiles, the bus rattled down the Great Hall Way. The windshield wipers slapped back and forth. The tires spun and skidded to the left and right. But gripping the steering wheel hard, Mr. Bus Driver kept the bus on course.

Through the driving rain—green, now blue, now violet—Bradley saw that they were passing the Grand Playground. Multicolored teachers slithered, wallowed, rolled, crawled, and did belly flops on the slippery asphalt. The entire surface had turned into one giant finger painting.

The bus roared past Teacherville, now painted bright green, and the white and chocolate milk dairy, which had turned dark blue. Every apple tree in the woods dripped orange and yellow.

At last the bus reached Mile 0 on the Great Hall Way. To Bradley's relief, Pedagog II still sat in the soccer field, bobbing up and down under the splattering paint.

"Can you fly that blimp, Mr. Bus Driver?" Bradley asked.

"If it has a motor, I can fly it," the man reminded him.

Three stout ropes tethered the blimp to the ground. During a lull in the rain Mr. Janitor sliced through them with his sickle while Bradley called to his class, "Come on, everyone. Let's get off the bus."

But no one moved.

"Hmm, they ate crab apples, didn't they?" said Prince Apple. "Ahh, I think they'll respond only to a teacher's command."

Bradley nodded, and in the deep, husky voice of authority that he had heard his teacher use hundreds of times, he said, "All right, stooodents. Form a straight line outside the bus."

In unison the class rose and marched off the bus.

"Stooodents, proceed onto the blimp," ordered Bradley.

And his class stamped up the metal stairs. Miss Library, Miss Secretary, Prince Apple, Mr. Janitor, and Mr. Bus Driver quickly followed.

With his class and the others now safe, Bradley had one last task to perform. He ran to the woods and found a stick. Heavy gray rain had just fallen, and in the paint that covered the soccer field he wrote in giant letters:

BRADLEY WAS HERE

The instant Bradley leaped up the metal stairs, Mr. Bus Driver pulled a lever and the blimp rose off the ground. Soon it floated above the colorful rain.

Bradley looked out the window to admire the sloppy scene he had created. Paint covered every corner of the peanut-shaped island as on an artist's pallet. And still more paint spewed out of Chalk Mountain—black, then white, then turquoise, then peach.

"What a mess!" said Bradley. He knew Operation Misteach would be canceled, and all the schools in the world were saved. "What a glorious, glorious mess!"

The School Day Ends

As the blimp soared over the ocean, Bradley turned to his classmates. They sat silently in their seats, motionless, stuck in the crab apple trance.

"Will they ever snap out of it?" he asked the adult passengers, who sat behind him. "How will I explain this to their parents?"

Miss Secretary looked at the rows of blank faces with sorrowful eyes, and Miss Library said, "Sorry, Bradley, I never read the health and medical books in the Big Book Building."

"Kids just aren't kids when they're that quiet and still," said Mr. Janitor, and Prince Apple shrugged his shoulders.

All at once a voice next to Bradley said, "Good blimp ride. Told you this field trip would be great, Bradley, didn't I? Mrs. Gross isn't as bad a teacher as you said, right?"

Good old Duncan. Bradley's friend was bouncing in his seat, squashing his nose against the window, and elbowing Bradley in the ribs.

Bradley wanted to hug his pal, but he didn't. Instead, he returned a sharp elbow into his side. "So you don't remember, Dunc?" he said.

"Remember what?"

"Apple Island? The Chalk Mountain volcano? The crabby teachers?"

"Are you going on about that teachers stuff again?" said Duncan. "Teachers are teachers."

So it was true—Duncan had no recollection of what had just happened. He thought this was all just a pleasant field trip, a short blimp ride.

Little by little the blimp filled with the sounds of chattering, singing, giggling, bickering, and complaining. Little by little Bradley's class was returning to normal. No one seemed to care or even notice that Mrs. Gross was gone or that five other adults had joined them.

When the blimp landed at the airport, everyone piled out and boarded the yellow bus still parked across the runway.

Mr. Bus Driver drove the bus down the highway while the class sang, "One hundred bottles of beer on the wall, one hundred bottles of beeeeeeeeeeeeeer . . . ," as if they had never stopped.

Finally the bus pulled onto the school grounds and parked in front of the beige, L-shaped school building.

Bradley turned to his Apple Island friends. "This is it. My school," he said. "And, Prince Apple, by the front door is the principal's office. The secretary works in there too, Miss Secretary. Mr. Janitor, that man sweeping the sidewalk is our school janitor. And see that room on the corner, Miss

Library? That's our library."

BRRRIIIIIIIIIIIIIIIIIIIING!

School was out, and students came charging out the doors. Like parachuters out of a plane, Bradley's class leaped from the bus and scattered in all directions.

Bradley followed the grownups off the bus and faced them again. "But where will you go?" he asked. "What will you do?"

"Well, uh, we've just been discussing that very thing," said Prince Apple.

"Remember, Brad," said Mr. Janitor, "some crabby teachers have already come to this country. And one bad apple can spoil a whole school."

"So I'll drive this bus to every school in the country," said Mr. Bus Driver. "We'll search for any teachers with purple ankles."

"Maybe the boys and girls can help us," said Miss Secretary. "Anyone who is brave enough can check the color of their teacher's ankles, perhaps during story time."

"And we'll also visit the libraries," said Miss Library. "I'm going to make sure the crabby teachers haven't put any of their Operation Misteach books in them yet."

"Sounds great," said Bradley. "When do we leave?"

"Sorry, Brad," said Mr. Janitor. "You need to stay at your school and finish your education. We know you'll be doing more great things in the future. You're the apple of our eye."

After hugs and hearty handshakes, the former castaways climbed back onto the bus. As it rolled away Bradley turned toward his school.

"Well, so much for that school day," he said. "Now there're only four days until the week is through, twenty-seven weeks until the year's over, and eight years until I graduate."